A BROKEN JOURNEY

LAURENTIAN LIBRARY 36

A
BROKEN
JOURNEY

a novel by
MORLEY CALLAGHAN

MACMILLAN OF CANADA/TORONTO

© Morley Callaghan 1932

First published 1932

First Laurentian Library edition 1976
Reprinted 1978
ISBN 0 7705 1394 8

Printed in Canada for
the Macmillan Company of Canada Limited,
70 Bond Street,
Toronto, Ontario M5B 1X3

FOR
LORETTO AND MICHAEL

A BROKEN JOURNEY

THE middle-aged but vibrantly dominant Teresa Gibbons was in a jolly humor and talked freely as she drove to the station to meet her daughter Marion. Two or three times she tried to exchange sly glances with the young man leaning back in the cab beside her. But he was only half listening. Sometimes he frowned and sometimes he smiled with serene boyish pleasure at his own thoughts.

Hesitating a moment, Mrs. Gibbons said, "Aren't you listening to me, Peter?"

"I've listened to everything you've said."

"To every single word, eh, Peter?"

"Till just now, when I started thinking."

"Thinking of what?"

"Of seeing Marion again."

Shrugging her shoulders, Mrs. Gibbons sighed deeply and then went on talking. There were some people who thought her an unusually devout woman, and some thought her an old hussy beyond redemption. Those who thought her devout had possibly seen her hurrying to the Cathedral, with a severe, earnest expression on her face, and had seen her head bent soberly all through the mass. One time, at a solemn high mass on Christmas Eve, when the choir was accompanied by stringed instruments and the Archbishop's weak old voice sang the mass, she had been in a kind of rapture which had held her until the crowd had left the church and she had remained in her pew for many minutes as if filled with wonder at the exultation in her own soul. And everybody knew, of course, that she had wanted her daughter Marion to be a nun and had been joyful when she had become a novice at the convent only a few blocks west, near the park.

But there were other people—especially Mr. Gibbons' sister, the older, red-headed one, who followed the ponies—who thought Teresa Gibbons a sensual, materialistic woman without any morality, whose infidelity was a bit remarkable though ridiculous at her age. Mrs. Gibbons had been married twenty-three years. As a girl she had been hot-tempered, bursting with vitality and eagerness and strong emotions that sometimes sent the blood rushing to her head and left her dizzy. For two years she had been a good, faithful wife to Gibbons, and after that, for twenty years or more, though they lived in the same house, they could not tolerate each other.

For almost ten years she had been without any kind of a lover and had longed for affection from some one. She longed to be kissed and pampered and caressed, but couldn't bear the thought of trying to find a lover. During the war she drove a transport truck around the city and looked very dark, vivid, and handsome in her uniform. At the camp, just outside the city, she had met a young, fair-haired officer, who was at first a bit afraid of her because

she was so hot-tempered and impulsive, and he
simply couldn't believe his good luck when she
seemed to want him for her lover. To her he
seemed so extraordinarily clean and his emotions
were direct and honest. She thought of him all
the time and prayed earnestly to express her thanks
at being so happy. Her happiness seemed so fragile
that she was always afraid of spoiling it, and besides, at this time she wanted to be a good woman,
and used to think that in spite of the young officer's
feelings, he would be happier if they could arrange
a separation from her husband before they lived
together. So she would not let him make love to her.
All her nights were feverish with longing for him.
She seemed to be actually afraid to let the young
officer love her, as if afterward everything would
be lost.

The officer's regiment left for France. A few
months later he was killed. There had never
been any kind of union between them. If she
had only given herself to him she felt she might
have been able to stand losing him. She thought
herself the harshest, silliest woman in the world.
She went twice to Europe as a sort of peni-
tential pilgrimage; after that, when she decided she
had no other loyalty, she wanted to have a great
many lovers. It wasn't hard for such a woman with
money and a great deal of passion to attract a few
men. That was the way she got even with her husband for persecuting her. Even now, sitting in the

cab beside Peter Gould on the way to the station, she was telling about a quarrel she had had the night before with her husband; they had stood in front of each other taunting and hating. It was magnificent that they didn't strike each other; of course, that was the goal in the game, to see which one could provoke the other to an insane rage. "I talk to him quietly and keep smiling even when I'm helpless with rage," she said to Peter. "And he never smiles at all. He never lets a fresh expression flit across his face." She was able to resist her husband because he never really knew when he had hurt her, and she tried to keep her life going ahead, to keep everything mixed up and flowing ahead so he couldn't hurt her.

When they got out of the cab at the station Peter smiled as he watched Mrs. Gibbons smoothing her coat so she would look more impressive.

"We're a few minutes early," she said, taking a deep breath. "I wonder if Marion will be anxious to see us."

"Sure she will. And she won't be wondering how anxious we are to see her. She knows."

"I'll tell her what a sweet boy you've been, Peter. I don't know what I'd have done without you."

"If you'd sit down here," he said, "I'll go down to the tunnel and see if the train's on time."

Peter was the son of a retired country magistrate who had saved enough money to send one son to college and to the law school. His head was rather large and smooth, though when he perspired at all his hair curled a bit at the back. This large head along with the rather short neck and middle height had often worried Peter's father, who was of the same build and who had once had an attack of apoplexy; he was afraid that Peter, too, unless he was temperate in his way of living, might some day later on in life have the same kind of an attack. When Peter was younger his father had recited to him whole passages from the work of John Stewart Mill, the English libertarian, and his mother, before she died, had been in the habit of intoning the poems of Edgar Allan Poe; they wanted him to feel there was something beyond the business of getting along in a profession. And then, when it became clear that Peter was dreaming of a career at law, which would always find him a defender of human liberty, his father almost worshipped him. The only trouble was that in the meantime, before great causes could be defended, he had to earn a living, and in the law office where he worked he hardly made enough money to buy his clothes and pay his room rent.

As he passed through the station waiting-room he smiled cheerfully at the good-natured, freckle-faced woman with the ample bosom at the magazine stand. He got as far as the tunnel and looked up at the clock, intending to go back and sit down with Mrs. Gibbons, but instead he stood there with an eager, restless look in his blue eyes. Down by the tunnel, leading to the trains, he saw three different doors through which Marion might come. Again he looked up at the clock, shook his head, and tried to guess where he might see her first; at the first door, by the wall, or suddenly appearing in a crowd of people. And as soon as he thought of her face in a crowd, he remembered special times when they had seemed very close together, little moments at a theatre, or at a hockey game, or even on a crowded street at noon time when he could take hold of her hand and know that without saying a word they felt wonderfully close together. So he said to himself, "Come walking through that door down there, Marion. Come laughing and hurrying and I'll run up to you and kiss you. I can't wait here any longer." But all of a sudden he felt upset, and as he began to walk up and down the length of ten paces, he muttered, "She may not be on this train at all. She may have missed this train. How do I know?" It made him impatient and irritable as he went on walking up and down with a solemn expression on his face.

Then red-caps, loitering at the gate, rushed toward passengers who were coming through the tunnel. From the tracks below came the steady clanging of train bells. Peter saw Marion, slim and fair, coming toward him, walking with an effortless rhythmic swing, preceded by a porter who carried her bags. Just as she saw Peter and her mother, who was still some thirty feet away, she noticed, too, a young man beside her being greeted by an old woman who wiped her eyes and shook her head, and the young man, grinning, stood among his friends and took off his hat while they patted him on the shoulder. Marion smiled into the bare-headed young man's face, as though his enthusiasm delighted her. Then she rushed forward with both her little black-gloved hands held out to her own mother, who kissed her twice on each cheek.

Marion turned her head so she could smile at Peter, and she said, looking at his neat, slim figure, and at his pale-blue, fancy shirt, "Peter, well, I'm so glad, Peter." He held on to her hands, nodding happily, and trying to make her understand by the insistent motions of his head that he appreciated her elegance. She shook her own head with a child-ish pleasure in his admiration. They seemed to feel they were entirely alone in the station. Mrs. Gibbons was clearing her throat and Marion, glanc-ing at her, blushed slightly, the warm blood coloring her pale face, though her mother had only coughed abruptly.

"By the way, Peter, by the way . . ." Mrs. Gib-bons said. She cleared her throat again, for she did not want to appear ridiculous. "Shall we stand here," she said, "or shall we go on home?"

"Oh, let's talk here a while. It's so long since I've seen you, Mother, and you, too, Peter. It was a long trip. I came up the Pacific Coast and by the Great Lakes and through the rocky country on the north

shore of Lake Superior, those great cones of spruce
. . . the loneliest and most beautiful country in the
world. . . ."

"The main thing is you're home now," her mother
said.

"And we're glad of that," Peter added.

"How's your brother Hubert, Peter?"

"Fine. He'll be glad to see you."

"You'll be discouraged to know, Marion, that your
father's sister is hounding me for money," Mrs.
Gibbons said.

"Is she? I never liked her; she's a malicious
woman. Never mind, you're looking young and fresh,
Mother," Marion said, as they walked to the street
door.

Peter, smiling, followed a few paces behind.
Marion was walking with such a light step that her
mother, beside her, seemed to be putting her feet
down with extraordinary deliberation, though she,
herself, was a well-built woman. Once Marion
glanced back. The light shone on her teeth and
parted red lips. With a sober face Peter followed
the slight little effortless swing of her neat hips
and the even stride with the hips swinging so
gently away from the line of her upright body. And
when they passed out of the great doors to the street
and the strong afternoon sun shone all of a sudden
on the little tuft of fair hair by her ear and on the
side of her neck, he felt breathless with love for her.

The Gibbons family lived in a large, old brick

house on a side street off Jarvis, which had once
been a pretentious neighborhood, though now most
of the big houses had been turned into institutional
buildings.

In the house Marion's father was waiting to see
her. He was a skinny, hollow-cheeked man with long
drooping mustaches, wearing an English tweed Norfolk jacket. He had just come in from his stroll
across Queens Park, where he walked every afternoon in his jacket and slouch felt hat, carrying a
short, thick cane. He kissed Marion with a deliber-
ate, artificial enthusiasm, and at once began to talk
to Peter about a street meeting he had passed.
"Damn communists," he said. "They ought to clamp
them all in jail and most of the professors at the university, too. Teaching free trade and no tariff, little
better than sedition." Peter was looking at him
mildly, his chin drawn back as if he were apt to
laugh out loud at any moment, and Gibbons began
to think that Peter was finding him dull; whereas it
never occurred to Peter for a moment to take anything Gibbons said seriously, and he was merely
chuckling at the Norfolk sporting jacket and the oc-
casional throaty, cultured accent Gibbons used when
he wanted to be most impressive. Gibbons was anxious to express himself pompously, but Peter, by his
attitude, seemed to be reducing everything the man
said to its essentials, and so the fine sentences were
always ended lamely. At last Gibbons, who couldn't
stand being annoyed any longer by Peter's utter

complacency, shouted, "The country is going to hell, I tell you."

"Sure, it is. The market fell four points to-day," Peter agreed.

"What's that?"

"The market fell four points."

"Well, good God, man, doesn't it bother you? It's money to me. Do you want us all to begin over again?"

"Not at all. But if we did have a new beginning it mightn't be so bad. What you you think?" Peter said, trying to stir Gibbons up to a strong feeling of indignation. "If we began again," he said, "we could forget a lot of Old World sicknesses that have been brought over here, such as. . . ."

"Such as architecture, literature, the humanities and so on, I suppose," Gibbons said sarcastically.

"Sure. Anything that's worn too thin."

"And instead, we'd replace them with whatever you have in mind at the moment, eh?" Gibbons said, enjoying the note of irony he thought he had sounded. But Peter, with his head at an angle so the good side with the fine profile was turned to Gibbons, had a far-away look in his eyes as if he couldn't think of being serious about something that might be important to him: once indeed, he glanced at the sporting jacket and Gibbons' slouch felt hat and smiled, with his opinion more strongly confirmed.

Gibbons felt that Peter was laughing at him. He pulled the ends of his ridiculous, long mustaches. A few years ago when he had been an executive in the department store, he had amused himself by giving out hundreds of photographs of just his bare head and the mustaches to employees at Christmas time.

"Don't let Peter tease you, Dad," Marion said. "I'm going out to the garden. I'll be out there, Peter."

Gibbons, who was about to speak again, smiled coldly, implying with a shrug of his shoulders that Peter was absurd, and that Mrs. Gibbons was not to be overestimated at any time. He walked away as if he felt lonely in his own house.

"He isn't very amiable," Peter said.

"I didn't notice it," Mrs. Gibbons said sarcastically.

"It's my fault for riling him. Where did Marion go? Out to the garden?"

In the garden there was a small bench by a tree and a vine over some lattice work. Through the thick vine leaves Peter saw Marion's light dress. He walked softly on the green lawn toward the arbor. Outside, on the other side of the high painted fence, automobiles hummed on the macadam road. It was still quite light, hardly six o'clock, in the summer daylight saving time.

Marion was sitting on the bench, her blonde head held back against the green leaves, her throat long and arching. Her eyes were closed, but her red and moist lips were parting. In the shadows of the arbor her cheek bones seemed high and her skin was clear and fine. When she opened her eyes slowly and saw Peter looking at her, she moistened her lips with the tiny red tip of her tongue. Only the rich blood running in her cheeks and the faint movement of her lips revealed any agitation, for in her utter lack of movement and in the candid stare of her blue eyes there was a kind of calmness and poise that couldn't be disturbed.

"Thinking of what?"

"Thinking of you and liking you," she said simply.

"Your father doesn't like me."

"But I do. And anyway why should he? You laugh at him, and he thinks you're absurd."

"Maybe he's right. But I think he likes sparring around with me while we keep popping away at each other."

"Never mind, Peter, Mother likes you, doesn't she?"

"Evidently."

They were trying to make a conversation with easy words, but they were both disturbed and waiting. She leaned back on the bench and straightened out her legs with her ankles together. "Oh, dear," she said. "The seam in that stocking isn't straight. Don't you hate a girl when the seam in her stocking gets twisted and she looks bowlegged?" And she began to pull and twist the stocking while he watched her seriously. "There, that looks much better, don't you think, Peter?" she said, putting her ankles together again. The bench was back against the lilac tree and the leaves were so thick no one could see them from the house. Tall hollyhocks, pink and white, grew by the house. Fumbling for words, he intended to make some remark about the seam in her stocking, then he touched her shoulder with the tip of his finger and seemed to feel the warmth of her body underneath the dress.

"You seem so timid, Peter, you make me feel afraid," she said, bashfully.

"I'm just waiting. You said you'd tell me. You wrote me you would, I was talking about you with my brother last night and then I couldn't sleep at all. I'd think I was asleep and then I'd be wide awake, worrying about you and wanting us to be together. Maybe I was just shadow boxing with all the things in your life that might be stronger than me. I was worrying."

"But, Peter, I'm not afraid. I'm not afraid at all."

"Will you?"

"Yes," she whispered, trembling.

"Oh, Marion, I'll do anything you say. Anything. Anything."

Looking at him shyly and fearing he might think her too bold, she said, "We could get married at once without any one knowing about it, and then I thought we might go away together."

"I'm so lucky. Would you, would you really, Marion?" He leaned forward and began to talk with slow sincerity of the life they would have together; he began to tell her of his most secret plans and ambitions, as if his bright dreams were facts which

could be stated simply, and his whole soul seemed
to open up to her. Only half looking at him, she said,
"I thought we might go up to the Algoma Hills on
the north shore of Lake Superior. I was there two
years ago. There's an old, old village on a great river
called the Mission."

"A real mission?"

"No, Mission is just short for Michipicoten and
that's the name of the river. Please tell me, Peter,
you don't think me a hussy, do you? I was thinking
about it all the time I was away, though it seems
pretty bold for a girl to have figured it all out,
doesn't it?"

"No, no, no. But please let us hurry. Let us not
waste a minute. I feel if we delay at all everything
in the world will catch up to us."

"What in the world could catch up to us? That
country's so big and wild."

"When you're hiding something precious the whole
earth's too small. I just don't want to shorten the
time we'll have together."

"Peter, up there you'll have all the long days and
all the long nights."

"How do we know that will be long enough? We'll
hurry as if we didn't have a minute to spare."

Her eager simplicity made him humble and he
said, "We'll fix it all up. We'll get everything all
ready. We'll take a few days and get it figured out."
He held her hands and wanted to kiss her again.
But they were interrupted. Mrs. Gibbons, who was

standing a few paces away on the lawn, said with
surprise, "Marion, my dear." She was planted solidly
on the green lawn. Peter was startled; he felt that
Mrs. Gibbons was really astonished to think he
might want to love Marion. She had tried to speak
coolly but couldn't conceal her sudden resentment.
Her face looked red and heavy; she had the severe
expression of a resolute woman. Peter felt that Mrs.
Gibbons was angry at Marion with a sharp, personal
anger.

"Oh, dear, excuse me," Mrs. Gibbons said, smiling
and becoming more self-assured. "I'll go away and
not disturb you."

"Don't bother going, Mother."

"Bless you, bless the both of you. I'll leave you."

"On the contrary," Peter said, "I'm the one that'll
be beating it. I'm going to see my brother to-night."

"Tell him I'd like to see him," Marion said.

"Say, he'll want to see you. We talked about you
for hours the other night," Peter said.

Out on the street, he looked back once at the
house. He felt so sure of being loved, he didn't know
what to do with the surge of exhilarating energy inside him; he didn't know whether to loaf along the
street luxuriously, or start running with long strides.
Every time he passed a lamp post, he slapped it
with the palm of his hand. He felt an immense gen-
erosity toward two truck drivers out on the road who
were yelling at each other.

2

In the house Marion encountered her father, who was standing by the garden window with his hands deep in his pockets. He looked lean, pale and a bit tired. He had been upstairs in his own room packing his bags. The racing meet was over and he was going to follow the ponies to another city. All year he looked forward to the time when he could spend his evenings in hotels with hard-boiled trainers and politicians who were horse lovers, sitting on the bed or on the floor, the room filled with thick cigar smoke, all of them in shirt sleeves, their bald heads sweating as they drank Scotch highballs and told tall stories. While packing, he had thought with steady pleasure of being at the track in another city, and he had even stopped once, smoking his pipe thoughtfully, and wondered if he would ever come back; so he had muttered, "I'll have to kid the old girl a bit before I go anyway." Now he stood by the window, smiling at Marion. His feeling for her was vague and uncertain. If she had been the dead image of her mother, or if she had been boldly assertive, he would have hated her, but she was cool and quiet. "She probably thinks I'm an old tintype," he thought suddenly. With a kind of stubborn eagerness he wished he might have been a little closer to her; he wanted to say something to justify the life he led in the house.

"I'm tagging after the ponies to-morrow," he said. "Just as you come home, I go away. I never got the knack of making it pleasant around here for you, did I?"

"There was no trick required. I always liked my home."

"I mean, dash it all," he said, looking very flustered as he pulled at his mustaches, "I mean your mother and I haven't provided an idyllic background for you, have we?"

"It's been all right, Father."

He lowered his head to one side and took out his handkerchief, for he wasn't accustomed to expressing difficult emotions. "Your mother hardly likes me, that's putting it mildly, eh? I've done my best to put salt in her wounds. She's quite a woman, oh, yes, quite a soul. There was always a dash and go to her though. When we used to ride horseback together, she'd leave me far behind and make me uneasy, damn it. I mean it started a long time ago. I was so much in love with her and I was uneasy because I couldn't see why she should be in love with me, if you see what I mean, my girl."

"I know. But why should you. . . ."

"She was so damned handsome and gay in those days, too. I was a fool not to have trusted her. Do you understand what I mean? She made me uneasy because I couldn't imagine why she married me. So I've made a mess of things."

"No, you haven't made a mess of things. You've given us a fine home, and you've retired on your business success."

"Would to God I hadn't retired. There's nothing for me to do. I'm not really an old man, yet I've become quite useless. But I want you to understand about your mother and me. I married her and then like a first-class chump I was afraid of losing her, so I had to go and spoil everything. Of course, she has a bad temper, there's no doubt about that." He turned away as if he thought he might appear to be ridiculous. Then he blew his nose and and said, "I see you're fond of that young man, Peter."

"I am, and I'd like you to like him."

"He's all right. My generation amuses him, of course, but he'll get over that. He'll not get along in the world, though."

"Why?"

"He doesn't kick with the right foot. And he's a liberal and an optimist, and he doesn't know how out-of-date that is. He doesn't cater to people. You've got to taffy people to get along. He can't live alone. Oh, he's all right, though," he said, as if he couldn't bear to be drawn into a matter that didn't really interest him. "He amuses me, that's all," he said. He seemed weary as he walked away.

Marion stood there. Her thoughts were troubled. "Why do I feel so sorry for my father?" she thought.

"I've never thought about my father." She didn't hear her mother coming into the room.

"Good gracious, Marion," she said. "I can't help looking at you. Have we both changed so much, I keep on saying to myself? There you are a full-grown, elegant-looking woman. When you're around the house I still go on thinking you're a bit of a girl, but if you go away and then come back, I get quite a shock. I begin to wonder what's happened to everything and everybody. It's quite disturbing, dear."

"You look splendid, Mother; you look so full of life and so handsome."

"Handsome is a bad word, Marion. Young women are beautiful; older women are called handsome. But I do feel better than I've felt in years. That Peter is such a jolly fellow, isn't he? He seemed awfully glad to see you."

"I was glad to see him."

"I'm honestly glad you like him. I want you to like him."

"Would you go so far as to like to see me marry him?"

"Marry him, marry Peter, you marry Peter. Oh, Marion, child alive, Peter wouldn't think of that." She seemed disturbed beyond all reason and looked quite indignant.

"But if he should ask me?"

"Heaven bless us, dear, he won't ask you. Put such nonsense out of your head, especially when you're not in love with him." She leaned back, smiling with so much broad tolerance that Marion merely took a deep breath, blinked her eyes and turned away.

She went to her own room early in the evening, for she was tired, and she passed her mother's room, where the light would burn all night: it was a superstition with her mother that she might die in her sleep and she didn't want to die in the dark. Marion hesitated, then tapped on the door. As she listened, she remembered that her mother kept the light burning for another reason, too; her dreams interested her: when she woke up after a vivid dream she liked to lie there with light burning and speculate on the nature of her dream. Marion opened the door and saw her mother in a purple dressing-gown sitting on an easy-chair and glancing at all the newspapers with a pair of scissors in her hand. If she saw a headline of what might be an interesting account of a crime, tale of passion, an important wedding, or a great religious event, she marked the column and cut it out with the scissors and put it away with other collected clippings, all waiting to be read on some dull evening when she had nothing else to amuse her. Recently she had been reading nothing but historical novels with European settings, but there was a time when she had read hardly anything but the Lives of the Saints, and for hours she would sit rapt in her own fiery thoughts as she dreamed of martyred nuns who had cut off their lips and their noses so they would be so hideous their heathen captors would not want to deprive them of their chastity. Her favorite saint was Augustine, because his life had been so turbulent before he found peace, and she had read his *Confessions* four times. But the only books she had never tired of reading were those on the small table by her bed, her manuals on the culture and care of roses.

Marion said to her, "I came in to say good-night, Mother. I never saw you looking so contented. Your hair is done nicely, too. Were you going out?"

"I had intended to but the time passed so rapidly just sitting here. I'm glad you're home and sleeping in the house to-night, Marion."

"Good-night, Mother."

"Good-night, dear."

As soon as she was in her own room Marion felt so alive and full of bliss she flung herself on the mauve silk bedspread and tried to bury her head deep in the pillow, and then it was delightful to mutter to herself, "I ought to take off that spread; I'll ruin it and it was given to me for a present, or I ought to kick off my shoes." She got up to fold the bedspread back. Then she sat down with her hands in her lap, undid her shoe straps, and with a solemn face kicked off first one shoe, then the other, to the farthest corner of the room, and giggled as if she had never been so amused in all her life. She wasn't thinking of anything at all, just letting herself feel happy. As she sat there she heard the soft tolling

of a bell, a faint silver tolling that hardly reached
her and seemed to come out of the clear, warm night,
and she remembered it was the bell in the convent,
four blocks west near the park, and next door to
Doctor Stanton's property, where she had actually
been a novice for a very short time. The tolling of
the bell . . . and she remembered swiftly. She had
not gone into the convent as a timid young girl.
After the university, when she was twenty-two, she
had begun to think of her mother's life as something
twisting and decaying at the very root within her
till she had become a demoralized woman. She
had thought also that a young woman ought to
be able to do something with her own life, and
a feeling which had been building up within her
grew large and came to a peak one day, and she decided eagerly that if she lived alone, say in a religious
order, she might find strength, intensity and courage.
Though she wanted to keep a deep respect for her
mother, she wanted at the same time to be utterly
apart and different from her, clean, simple and un-
touched by any of the passions she felt had destroyed
her mother. So she had become Sister Mary Rose, a
simple person, in a world where there were many
rich consolations. The novices at recreation hour
used to walk by the high brick wall dividing Doctor
Stanton's property from the convent garden and
whisper sincerely that soon the Mother Superior's
prayers would be answered and the doctor sell his
house to her. The old brick house was between the

convent and the edge of the park. For five years the
Mother Superior had been trying to buy it from the
bigoted old man to use it as a residence. Once the
Mistress of the Novices had asked them all to pray
that the doctor, who had declared definitely that his
old home would never become a part of such an in-
stitution, might be persuaded to change his mind.
God was often more willing to grant favors when
the prayers came from fresh, eager young souls. And
Sister Mary Rose, who had been a novice for only
a few weeks, was determined to endure all the hard-
ships till she one day would become a nun. She
had looked charming in the habit with the little
black cape of the novices, and she was having none
of the pain and troubles of some of the others. She
ate the plain food hungrily; she got to like immensely the well-buttered slice of bread they had at
collation hour in the morning; her body ached at
first from the hard bed, but, to herself, she insisted
that she didn't feel the pains, and refused, unlike
some of the others, to stretch her pillow out lengthwise, and sleep on it. And she had prayed and prayed
and prayed that Doctor Stanton sell the property to
the convent, till at last he had died. . . . The bell
was no longer tolling. "What an earnest young lady
I must have been just such a few years ago," she
thought, laughing out loud to herself. She got up
from the chair and walked over to the window in her
stockinged feet and looked out across the street at
Doctor Wilton's house. While she was looking across

the road Mrs. Wilton came out with a fat and lazy
cat at the end of a long string, and she walked up
and down in front of the house. The Wilton's, of
course, had no children. "Oh, dear, I wish I had
some new clothes. It was so hot out to-day," Marion
thought; but she knew she could no longer avoid
having thoughts that made her breathless. Only half
undressed, she threw herself on the bed again and
closed her eyes tight. Crouching on the bed, she put
her hands on her temples. The steady pumping of
her heart was so disturbing and delightful, she could
hardly stand it.

As she sat up, she thought it would be good to go
down and attach the garden hose to the tap and
water the back lawn while she sat on a chair and was
sprayed by cool water swishing on the grass. She
rumpled and tousled her fair hair all over her head.
Then she noticed a small run at the top of her long
stocking and was so concerned, she pressed a wet
finger on the place to stop the run. With indifference she changed her mind and made the run go the
whole length of the stocking. Laughing, she pulled
off the stocking and looked at her bare foot critically.
Eagerness was so strong within her that she tried to
stop thinking of Peter. At last she got into bed,
turned out the light and began to think of the blue
Algoma Hills, the great lake, the black rocks, the
high, overhanging crags of basalt and the sunlight
on miles and miles of burnt timber, solitary, dried
out, sun-white stumps with the roots in the surface

earth on great rocks. She thought of herself and
Peter going up the river in a boat to the Mission,
and going up the steep bank to Bousneau's boarding
house, the only boarding house for miles and miles.
They would have a clean, whitewashed room over-
looking the river.

But before she could fall asleep, Ag, the maid,
rapped on the door lightly to ask if she would like
a bit of lunch. "There's some cold chicken," she said.
"How would you like some with a glass of your
mother's white wine?"

"Come on in, Ag," Marion said, sitting up in bed.
Ag was standing in the lighted doorway, a short,
dark, plain-looking girl with small black eyes.
Against the light her body looked squat, her head
square, as she tried to intimate that she was willing
to go out of her way to please Marion. Ag had
been with the family a number of years. Whenever
there was a dispute in the house between Mr. and
Mrs. Gibbons, she sympathized with him. To herself, she used to think that he was an aloof, em-
bittered, honorable man who had been unhappy in
his marriage, a very lonely man who wanted affection for some one. Ag was resentful of Teresa
Gibbons, and sometimes looked at her, after there
had been a quarrel, as though she would growl at
her. She felt, too, that because she, herself, had no
lovers or intimate companions, there was a kind of a
bond between her and Gibbons. When Gibbons urged
her to spy on his wife who was entertaining other

men, she felt closer to him, and when they whispered together, watching Mrs. Gibbons, Ag used to glow with eager satisfaction because she was close to this man who trusted her. There was also the sister, Elizabeth Gibbons, the red-headed sporting lady, who, being anxious to know all about the family affairs, used to invite Ag to come and see her and have a cup of tea in the afternoon while they talked about Teresa Gibbons. Ag had told Marion how much she liked Elizabeth Gibbons for making her laugh and putting her arm around her affectionately; Ag would have talked for hours to try and express her admiration for the lean sporting lady with her henna-tinted hair, her mascaraed eyes and her cigarette hanging loosely from her very red lips. Ag felt that when she was with this woman, she was close to some one who was reckless, vital, extravagant, who would never grow old. And since she had to express her admiration to some one who would be sympathetic, she used to wait till Marion went to bed in the evening and then put her in good humor by bringing her a snack to eat.

"Have you missed me much, Ag?" Marion said.

"I was hoping you'd let me fetch you something to-night," Ag said very simply. "I'm glad to see you."

"Why, you're a dear girl. I'll light the light and wait here in bed for you."

A few minutes later Ag returned with the plate of thin, buttered bread and slices of chicken breast and the glass of white wine.

"Have you been happy, Ag? Having much fun?"

"Fairly happy, Miss," she said carefully.

"You're not thinking of getting married, surely?"

"Oh, no. Imagine you saying that. I wouldn't do such a thing."

"Never mind, Ag. Don't get indignant. I'm just kidding you. Come on, tell me if there's any news."

"I suppose you know your father is going away to-night."

"He is, is he? Why he hardly mentioned it. Where is he going?"

"Following the horses, I guess. He enjoys it, you know."

"I wonder if he'll say good-by to me. Oh well. . . . Has Peter been around here much to see mother? Is she still worried about business matters and needing consolation and expert advice?"

"She phones Mr. Gould, and he comes often in the afternoons. She's very fond of him," Ag said almost to herself, as though afraid of offending Marion.

"Is my mother very fond of him? I mean does she really like him," Marion said, smiling. Suddenly she began to laugh out loud, laughing so hard her shoulders shook. Hastily Ag removed the tray from the bed and began to laugh too. They sat together on the bed laughing, Marion leaning far back, her white throat curving, her chin moving slightly from side to side. "Oh, Ag," she said, putting her white hand on Ag's arm and drawing her closer to her. Ag, who was laughing almost hysterically, put her head down on Marion's shoulder; her round blunt nose was pressed against the soft nape of Marion's neck; her wide lips moved warmly as she pressed harder against the neck, and Marion, smiling now, patted her head. All of a sudden Ag began to cry. Tears from her eyes fell on Marion's bare shoulder. Ashamed, she stood up. "Oh, please, please forgive me. You're so lovely. I'm glad to see you. But we oughtn't to laugh. And it seemed so dreadful about Peter Gould coming to see your mother that I couldn't help feeling bad."

"But why does he come to see mother so often," Marion said, as she stared at Ag.

"She phones him. She just has to talk about business matters, though I've noticed she gets that over pretty quick. Then she gets so sweet with him. I just had to tell you."

"Ag, listen to me. Just what are you trying to tell me?"

"I'm just telling you what I know. I've seen her. He puts his arm around her. I've seen them together and I can't help looking. And when he's here, she's so delighted, and when he's gone she stands at the window watching him and puffing and sighing till it makes me sick. And I hope you don't think me forward."

"You mean. . . . Oh, you can't mean that she loves him."

"I do. And I'm dead sure of it."

"Does he . . .?"

"I don't know what he thinks, but I know it's

such a pleasure to her, and I've thought it a shame to see her taking your sweetheart like that. You don't mind me mentioning it, do you?" Ag said, whispering eagerly.

"Oh, no. No. Thanks, Ag," she said vaguely.

"Well, good-night, Miss."

"Good-night, Ag. You're a dear girl."

As soon as Ag closed the door Marion threw off the covers and sat up in bed, intending to get up at once. Then she fell back, inert and bewildered. A few moments ago she had been so full of bliss that even her slightest thoughts had seemed deliciously exciting: there had seemed to be such a sweet, intimate pleasure in just waiting to fall asleep. But now she was wide awake, only her body was heavy. She tried to subdue the excitement that was making her breathe so jerkily. She was trying to keep herself from rushing into her mother's room, waking her, and shouting with anger. This feeling, making her so restless, was even stronger than her feeling of shame and disgust. "I won't believe it. I won't till I speak to her to-morrow," she muttered. She was holding herself so tightly, she thought if she didn't fall asleep something would break inside her.

3

BUT she went out in the morning without speaking
to her mother and stayed out all day. "What can I
say to her? I don't know what to say," she thought.
In the afternoon she went into the grocery store
owned by the Italian, Badame, who also owned a
racehorse that sometimes won when the odds were
heavy against it. She leaned across the counter,
talking lazily with Badame and with his wife, whose
dress was so loose at the throat, whose skin was so
milky and soft. Customers coming into the store
stared at Marion, wondering why she laughed so
huskily at the bare-armed storekeeper by the pile of
oranges. Moistening his heavy red lips, Badame said
his horse, Estaban, was all set for to-morrow. If
anything intervened in the meantime, he would
phone her, he said. She gave him a ten-dollar bill
and he promised to play it across the board.

In the evening Ag looked at Marion with pity and
told her Peter had phoned three times, so Marion
said to herself, "I'll speak to mother this minute,"
and she went to her mother's bedroom and saw her
standing by the dressing-table, smiling to herself as
she gently rubbed the tips of her plump fingers on
her slightly wrinkled neck. A slight new wrinkle was
requiring all her attention; she leaned closer to the

mirror; her hair was pulled back from her head and tied in a knot so it wouldn't disturb her sleep.

Marion sat down on the bed and said, "Hello, Mother. Are you doing anything? I just felt like talking. I was wondering when father might come back. I was thinking he's a shy man even with his own family."

"He didn't say when he'd be back. I might have asked him, but you know, I felt downright uneasy all the time he was talking to me. He seemed so patient. Your father is never very patient."

"If he gets the notion, he'll probably go from one track to another before he gets tired and comes home, don't you think so?"

"I wouldn't bet a red cent on it, because he kept on smiling at me. Something was on his mind."

"He was talking to me about Peter. Peter's been around here quite a bit, eh?"

"Now and again. He works for me, darling, you know, and I'd like to see him get along in his profession and I believe I could help him." She smiled, and Marion began to tremble.

"Does he come often?"

"Mainly in the afternoons when he's tired of being downtown."

"He probably finds you mighty jolly company, Mother."

"I want him to like me."

"Mother, Mother, listen to me. You know I love Peter. I don't know what to say to you. I can't find anything to say. Just listen to me, Mother. Don't you see what I'm thinking and what I'm feeling?" Her neck was arched as she leaned across the bed with her blue eyes wide open. "I would never deliberately hurt you, Mother."

As though perplexed by her own feelings, Mrs. Gibbons got up and walked away slowly. "You're still just a child, Marion. I wouldn't hurt my own flesh and blood, would I? I say a little prayer for you every night, three Hail Marys, so God will make you happy." Then she added with shy sincerity, "I know Peter doesn't love you. I'm sure of that, girl. I know I'll never be able to explain how I feel about it, I can tell that by the way you're staring at me." As she glanced uneasily at Marion, a slow flush reddened her face as though she were ashamed. "A girl who has become a young woman can't imagine her mother being so much in love with any one that she'd die for. . . ."

"Mother, darling, you're only trying to tease me, aren't you?"

"I'm not, Marion. You say that to hurt me."

"I'm not trying to hurt you. It's absurd, absurd."

"Why is it? Just because you can say fiddlesticks?" she asked, looking very upset.

Marion took a deep breath and said huskily, "Then you're honestly suggesting, Mother, that Peter . . . that Peter is attracted to you?"

"I think so," she whispered.

"You think so?"

"Yes."

"But you can't believe that. Oh, Mother, look at me."

With surprising vigor and dignity, Mrs. Gibbons said, "I tell you to your face I don't feel absurd. I don't feel small and mean. I feel big and strong and eager about it." Then she changed as though frightened and began to plead, "Look at it in this way, Marion. You're a young woman. You'll have a chance to have all kinds of men in love with you. But Peter is so very precious to me. The other night I went down to the Cathedral to pray and then on the way I walked in a dream and kept looking up at the stars. I was all mixed up and worried but I knew I was happy. You know I never had any happiness with your father. Year after year I've been hoping for so much, too. Now when I think Peter will be the last thing on earth I want, you wouldn't spoil it, would you? You're a young, good-looking girl." She held her breath, remained upright for one moment, and then as her shoulders slumped, she began to cry quietly. She was crying like a woman whose sorrow comes out of tenderness for some one she loves. Tears weren't running on her cheeks, but her eyes kept filling up with tears.

"Please, Mother, don't cry, don't cry like that, Mother."

"I'll stop. But I'm not crying, Marion. Only don't be angry about Peter, will you? If you were angry and you wanted to, you could take him."

Her mother's fumbling sincerity filled Marion with shame. "Don't worry," she said, "I'll never, never, compete with you."

"I can hardly hear what you're saying."

"Can't you? I'm saying you don't love me at all. You're a sinful woman. You'll spoil my life, but I won't do anything. I won't raise my little finger."

"How can I spoil something that isn't really there?" Mrs. Gibbons said mildly. "It's you that ought to leave me alone," she added, trembling with eagerness to be convincing and reasonable.

"All right. I will. What are you going to do?"

"Nothing, nothing at all, Marion."

She spoke so confidently that Marion was filled with hot resentment. White-faced, she drew her knees up under her on the bed. She got up with her head pushed forward a bit and both her fists clenched as though to fight off something, and she walked over to her mother. She felt big with contempt. Her mother was leaning back with one hand up to her face as though expecting a blow.

Then Marion felt a bit dazed. Coming through the open window, she could smell the full scent of the blooming garden roses. The roses were splendid this year, the best year for roses in a long time, according to her mother, who was spending more time in the garden than ever before, clipping and pruning and tending each bush she knew so well. Twelve years ago she had planted the rosebushes around the fence and made a border for the whole garden.

No gardener working on the lawn dared touch them. In the fall she would clip the rotten wood and spray the bushes and cover them with bagging. In the spring she would go out and watch seriously for the first buds. Only last year a painter working on the back veranda had let his ladder fall on one yellow rosebush and had broken it at the root, and she had cried all morning as she heaped earth around it. The scent of roses on the still and heavy night air came through the open window. "It's incredible. I'll not believe it. I'll not believe I'm jealous of my own mother. How can you feel there is any honor or decency left?" she asked.

"I love Peter. Why should it be incredible that I love him?"

"There's no reason why, I suppose. You don't think he encouraged you, do you? You can't believe that he did."

"Oh, yes, he did," Mrs. Gibbons said with earnest conviction. And Marion muttered, "I hate him, I hate him for doing anything at all to make it like this."

"What are you saying, Marion?"

"Nothing. I was just thinking out loud."

"What were you thinking?"

"I said nothing. But it doesn't matter whether I believe you or not, does it?"

"If you don't believe me I'll feel wretched and evil. You must believe me."

"I believe you," Marion said wearily.

She sat erect on the bed, staring at the window, hearing nothing. She never moved. She seemed to be alone where she dared make no sound. Then Mrs. Gibbons, who couldn't stand the silence any longer, said loudly, "What are you looking at, Marion?"

"I'm just looking out the window."

"What are you going to do?"

"I think I'll go out for a while."

"But it's going to rain."

"I don't mind the rain."

"Then be sure and take your umbrella," Mrs. Gibbons said, as if it had become of extraordinary importance that Marion should not get caught in the rain.

For a moment, in her own room, Marion hardly moved, remembering times when Peter had teased her mother by putting his arm around her. "How many fellows haven't done the same thing to mothers of their girls?" she thought. Then, without any warning from within, she threw herself face down on the bed and began to cry; her whole body, which was held so taut, now shook with helpless grief. She was crying so hard, she couldn't get her breath. She thought she would choke. She rubbed her face on the pillow. It was dark in the room and dark outside. As she gasped for breath, she heard her mother moving along the hall, the heels of her mules flopping loosely on the floor. Marion turned over and lay heavily, looking up at the ceiling and, as she sighed and thought she would cry again, she muttered, "Mother is jealous of me and looking at me and thinking I have an advantage because I'm younger, and then she's envious. No matter what Peter thinks, he must have encouraged her, and I couldn't stand to think I took the lover my mother wanted with the two of us in the same house, waiting and hating each other." Marion thought she was being realistic and reasonable, but within her, welling up from the dark world in her thoughts, where every floating image seemed to quicken her pulse and pull at her heart, she felt a sudden jolt of jealousy. Crouched and trembling, with her hair falling down over her face, she muttered, "God Almighty, I'll never let my own mother be jealous of me, I'll never be jealous of her." She had tried to live in a world far beyond her mother's sensualism, and had even gone to a convent to devote herself to the eternal Virgin that it might be a symbol for her life. But now, by the looseness of her passion, her mother had drawn her into her life till they both wanted the same man. "Everything I've wanted is now destroyed utterly," she thought.

She went over to the leaded window and looked out. Everything was very quiet and still. It was time for the full moon, but instead it looked like rain. Then she sat down on her hope chest by the window and wondered what she had ever done to her mother that she could have so little affection for, her. As she clutched the edge of the chest with her fingers, she remembered that in it were all the little keepsakes she had cherished since she had been a girl; there was an old picture of her standing by the great oak tree. In those days, years ago, her mother had been sweet to her. It had been Marion's birthday and the children were having a surprise party for her, and her mother had taken her walking in the park so she wouldn't know, and had taken the picture of her standing by the oak tree. That day she had worn her best alice-blue frock; before they had gone out together she had gone to her mother's room and from a bureau drawer taken the transformation or "switch" as she called it, that her mother used when she wanted to pile her hair high on her head: the "switch," of course, was black, but Marion, who had been disappointed that her hair wouldn't grow faster, had tried to pin the black switch under her blonde hair so it would make a big bun at the back. When her mother saw her she had hugged her tightly and nearly died of laughter. But that was years ago, before her mother's life had become distorted and ugly.

Putting on her loose, light coat and without bothering about a hat, Marion went out to the street and began to walk up to the car tracks on Bloor Street and West. It started to rain lightly. As soon as she felt the first drops she said to herself, like a little girl who remembered her mother's advice, "I ought to have brought an umbrella." But she was blocks away from the house. She thought she was hating Peter. Her heart was beating too hard. She put her hand over the place to stop it. "There's no use thinking much about it," she said. "I've made up my mind." The wind was getting much stronger, blowing back her hair from her forehead, sweeping the rain across the street, and slanting it under rows of street lights with rainbow halos around them. The dark wet pavement glistened and small pools of water formed in the indentations on the road. With her hands deep in her pockets, Marion went down the street to the corner, past old buildings with long, caving roofs. She was standing on the corner by the barber shop with the long plate glass window and the white lights. A torn awning flapped in the wind. She looked through the window at three white-coated barbers, their backs to the window, and through the open door came the sweet scents of rich spices, heavy hair oils, soothing powders and faint perfumes. Through the streaming wet window she saw a squat Italian rubbing his hands through foamy white lather on the head of a man in the chair. Her own face felt hot, though the rain was beating against it. She liked the feel of the rain. The top of her head felt wet. A kind of deep contempt for all her old notions and opinions was bewildering her, and she muttered, "Peter was rotten. Anyway, I'm not thinking of him at all."

At the corner, under the light, gasoline had been spilled from an auto and it colored the dark pavement brilliantly, great blotches of high color, gleaming like a peacock's tail. Marion crossed the road, loafing along, a woman walking in the rain with no definite place to go. As she passed the restaurant on the opposite corner, three young Jews and two heavy, fair men looked at her appraisingly, and, because a policeman was standing across the road in a doorway, they only whistled, then shrugged their shoulders and called, soft and coaxing, "Blondie, blondie, come in out of the rain." The coaxing voices, calling after her and desiring her, reminded her of the boys who had wanted to love her when she was at the university. They had kissed her and she had wanted them to hold her tightly. There was a fellow named Christopher, a tall boy with blue-black hair, who made her tremble in his arms when he was leaving her in the evenings after dances. At that time she had become aware of her mother's infidelities and of the men who came openly to see her, and her own virginity became very precious to her. To find herself in a different world from her mother's, she had become a novice in the convent, where her ardor to try serious contemplation used to startle her. With delight she had read of the ecstasies of St. Teresa of Avila, who had so much love in her heart that she went straight to the image of her Lord. One night, before going to sleep in her cell, when her back was aching from the hard board, she had tried to lift herself into an ecstasy so she might see the image of Christ and feel Him beside her before she went to sleep. Sometimes she was able to see the slender form of a young man, and she shivered with exultation, but dared not tell other novices for fear the Mother Superior might question her. One night she could not sleep; she longed to see the image again. Before she feel asleep the image was in her head so clearly, she almost cried out, for she recognized the tall boy, Christopher, who used to hold her in his arms. She cried all night, for she knew she ought to leave the convent. "It's my mother's nature in me," she thought at the time.

As she stood on the corner, looking across the street, with drops of rain falling on her throat and trickling in tiny rivulets down her neck, she had a sudden chaving for affection and sympathy.

A taxicab, with wheels licking the wet pavement, passed slowly and stopped a few paces ahead. After paying the cabman, a young fellow without a hat on bowed to him ceremoniously, and as soon as the car moved away, he smiled to himself and sat down with absurd contentment in a pool of water by the curb. He turned down his collar as though quite comfortable. He put his elbows on his knees and closed his eyes. Marion was only a few feet away from him, where she could see his fair, curly hair, his white, fine face, and a heavy blue welt over his eye. He was about eighteen.

He looked so helpless, getting so wet, and he seemed so simple in his contentment, that Marion was suddenly full of compassion for him. She forgot her own trouble. Timidly, as she approached, she said very gently, "You'd better get up and go home, or the policeman will take you to the station. Don't you think so?"

"Excuse me, oh, excuse me," he said, standing up and very nearly succeeding in bowing formally. "I hope I'm not embarrassing you. I was just resting. But lady, what are you walking around without a hat on for? You'll get your death of cold, really." He looked at her with so much honest regard for her health she couldn't help smiling. "You'd better go home," she said.

"You walk with me," he said with almost childish, trusting friendliness. Then, becoming more severe, he said, "It's not a laughing matter. You'll get cold and die of consumption." With the rain falling on his bare head, he wanted to stand there and lecture her.

"Come on, I'll go down as far as the corner with you," she said, smiling at him and liking him.

"Well, all right, but I'm going to look after you. You're pretty nice, you know." He held on to her arm firmly as though she were a lost young girl and he had found her and was taking her home to her mother. He was not tall and he walked erect. "I'll leave you here," she said, when they were at the corner. "No, no, no," he said. "I just live at the corner here. I have an apartment on the ground floor. Please come in and take off those wet shoes, please, lady."

"No," she said nervously, looking around, but

when he pleaded and seemed so harmless, she shrugged her shoulders. "Go on in like a good boy," she said to him. When he took hold of her arm, she only half resisted.

"I'd better not go in," she said.

"You're absurd, lady, simply absurd. What's your name?" he said, fumbling in his pocket for the key.

"Marion."

"That's a splendid name. I like you and your name, lady, really I do."

They went into a big front room and he turned on the light. The room was comfortably furnished, the walls papered plainly; many book shelves, piles of magazines on a long table, one deep easy-chair, and a long couch.

As he took off his coat, he kept on looking at her as though she were a reluctant patient and he was the doctor. In his shirt sleeves he began to move about the room, "Now, let me see," he said. "What ought I to do first of all?" Smiling, he smoothed back his short curly hair. "I know. I'll take off your damp shoes," he said brightly. She couldn't help liking his sympathy and his eagerness to be good to her. "What a lovely boy you must be when you're sober," she said with delight as he knelt down on the floor and began to loosen her shoe laces. Looking up with his very deep blue but very sunken eyes and his pinched white face, he said gravely, "Marion, I've been drunk for days. I'm specializing in Greek and Latin. I'm a classical scholar. But excuse me, perhaps you don't care for Ovid or Catullus. Sometimes I do and sometimes I don't, though I hardly ever go back on Catullus. I haven't done anything about either one for four days, though, of course, I'm sober enough now."

He placed her two shoes together on the rug and said, "Lady, your feet are wet." He was holding her small white foot. "My goodness," he said, "your legs are soaking. Your stockings'll simply have to come off."

Laughing, with embarrassment, she tried to resist while he kept repeating, "I'll put a pair of my socks on your little feet and we'll dry yours on a rad." He tried to help her undo her garters and peel off her stockings. Her face was crimsoning and she was flustered.

He leaned back cross-legged on the floor and looked with wonder at her slender white legs. "Such pretty, pretty legs," he said. "A lady like you coming right in here out of the rain with such pretty white legs."

"You're such a nice, romantic boy," she said, growing uneasy.

"Of course I am, of course," he said.

Then he looked at her as if seeing her for the first time. He sat down beside her and put his hand on her shoulder. The whole evening all of a sudden seemed to tire her; she was too tired even to be ashamed, and closing her eyes, she wilted. His breath was on her neck as she waited, but he was only heavy against her, and finally, when she began to feel cramped, she opened her eyes and saw his head drooping. His damp hair had been against her cheek. He was falling asleep with his lips parted and his face looking tired and thin.

Pushing him away gently, and putting a pillow under his head, she reached for her stockings and pulled them on, feeling the damp chiffon chilling her. She began to tremble and cry softly. Her shoes were still wet. She had a hard time putting her left arm in the sleeve of her coat. Looking around the room, she saw his overcoat on a chair and she put it gently over him. Listening, she could not hear the rain on the window. Once she knelt down beside him and kissed him on the lips. Then she went out.

The rain had stopped, and wind was drying gray patches on the dark pavement. It was cool. The clouds were opening, a few stars were shining in inky blotches and she caught a glimpse of the full moon riding high behind the rim of a cloud. Clouds seemed to be racing across the sky, parting, merging, and showing the dark rifts with shining stars. In the gutters the water was running steadily to the drains leading down to the lake. It had been a very wet night and in all the streets there was the sound of running water cleaning the streets and flowing into the great drains. Gutters were running with water all over the city.

As she began to walk home, Marion murmured, "Thank God nothing happened," for by now she was feeling cold, and she had only contempt for herself. There was such a fine city quietness in the street she hoped for a moment that nothing had happened at all that evening and she had been dreaming. The more she thought of it, the more unreal the night became. The streets were long. The moon was full. All the houses on the street were the same color in the bright moonlight, block houses put down neatly in a row, all the same size in the moonlight. It was so much like one of the bright pictures one remembers after a dream. The other parts of the dream gradually emerge and shape themselves around the few bright pictures that come easily. Just after she passed the corner, out of an alleyway came a grayish mongrel dog, mostly fox terrier, its head down close to the sidewalk, smelling her footsteps and looking doubtful. When she was at a street light, she turned and said, "Beat it, scat." But the dog stood there on the pavement, five paces away, looking at her dumbly with its head on one side and wagging its tail, and as she moved forward, the dog followed timidly to let her get a few paces ahead. They were both going along in the moonlight on the wide asphalt street. Marion wanted to encounter some one, but she heard only the patter of the mongrel's paws on the sidewalk as it limped along behind her. When she heard no sound at all, she felt alone and very tired. Turning, she wondered where the dog had gone, and saw it ten paces away with its hind leg lifted gracefully, its head turned, relieving itself against a post. She waited for the dog to catch up to her. "Hello, Pup. Hello, Pup," she said, taking a great fancy to it. A man and a girl passed under the light without looking at her and she had a ridiculous feeling that no one on the streets that night could see her; the fellow and the girl walking under the light were as unreal as the picture of the row of houses—all the same pale pastel shade in the moonlight.

But she was so chilled in her damp clothes, and so weary with disappointment in herself, she made up her mind to go into the first restaurant, a Chinese one near the corner of Bloor and Yonge, and have a cup of coffee. The dog followed her inside and crouched underneath the table, and when she noticed it, she smiled with delight, and asked the waiter to put a plate of bones under the table. As soon as she sipped the hot coffee, she tried hard to think she had exaggerated everything. She heard the dog tearing at the bones underneath the table.

At home her mother and Ag were asleep. Only the one light, which was always there at night time, was burning in her mother's room. First, she lay on the bed without undressing, her face pressed against the pillow, her heels held high up in the air. Then, as she got up and began to undress, she opened the window wide. The bell was tolling blocks away, over near the park. Streaks of moonlight shone on the garage roofs and farther away it shone on the housetops, and away down the sloping street, moonlight tipped the peaks of tall towers, tapering, receding, slanting up clean and firm. In a kind of stupor of nervous relaxation she lay down and tried to pray, but only said softly, finding the words delicious, "Dear Jesus," and could go no further, for she seemed to have forgotten how to pray. A chill calmness was in her. She felt she could see her whole life with intense clarity. She had been disappointed, then disgusted and revolted, had found it necessary to let herself be picked up by a little drunk and had waited for him to make love to her, which indicated clearly that unless she hung on to herself, she was apt to become a sensual little bawd. "Mother and I are just like each other. We're a pair and it would have been just like her to think of running off to a primitive country with a fellow like Peter when she was my age."

She got up and went out to the hall. Full of a strange, hurting compassion, she listened outside her mother's door. Her mother was asleep. This new tender loyalty to her mother, after her own resentment had tired her, puzzled her. "Poor Mother, forgive me for not trying to understand you," she whispered. She went back to her own room and, lying down, she seemed to be taking herself apart and finding only what was weak and pitiable. When she got into bed, her lips were moving in supplication for contentment and purity, but when she hunched up her knees, she felt within her an uneasy twinge of resentment.

4

WALKING along the street with his brother, Hubert, on their way over to the Arena to see the wrestling matches, Peter explained that he was going away with Marion and he was seeing her in a few hours so they could make arrangements for the trip. Hubert, who was taller and heavier than Peter, had a round face with smooth, rich-blooded cheeks and straggly black mustaches. He was walking with his big heavy body leaning forward, his left foot turning in with every step, and listening with as much alert enthusiasm as if he expected to go away with a beautiful girl of his own. He looked like a big, eager-faced boy bursting with startling information that was held back by his inner shyness, a big, strong fellow who seemed to find a strange exultation and happiness in his own life. Often he looked like a bum. At this time he wasn't working, so he was wearing a pair of Peter's shoes, one of Peter's ties, and his pouch was full of his brother's tobacco. The brothers tried to share everything in common, just as they went everywhere together. They played a fine game of tennis together and Hubert sang in a strong tenor voice when Peter played the banjo. Their father had had only enough money for one of them to go to the university, so Hubert had gone north to the lumber camps and the mines, and out West for the harvesting, feeling the sinister quality of the northern country and getting his own calmness and curious contentment out of it. Peter talked to Hubert about Marion as if only his brother could understand how happy he would be with her. They talked confidently and intimately as if they were both walking securely on a high upland where there was cool air and sunlight.

"If the rasslers, the big apes, look too phoney, I'll leave early and walk up to your place and wait for you," Hubert said.

"You could wait with Izzy Klein in the next apartment, if he's in."

In the Arena the brothers stood in the gallery in the cheap seats with little old red-faced men, husky laborers cursing richly, fat sporting men with hands thrust deep in their pockets, negroes, wops and limeys whose faces quivered with excitement. For a few moments the brothers watched the bouts, then again they began to talk about Marion as if they both had been thinking about her all the time. It might be better not to tell their father about her for maybe a year, they agreed, for Peter really couldn't afford to get married. Hubert, grinning enthusiastically, had his arm around his brother's shoulder. Peter was very grave, like a man who wants to appear casual about a matter that is actually of desperate importance to him. His eyes were shining with an excitement that couldn't be touched or disturbed by the cheering crowd around

him, though he was staring down at the pyramid
of white light shining on the heavy sprawling
wrestlers. Suddenly he smiled with an expression
of extraordinary serenity and said to his brother,
"You've at least crossed through that Algoma
country where we're going. What's it like? What'll
I need to take?" Hubert said, "I don't know about
down by the lake, but further north, where the train
goes through, it's a country of coal-black rock.
Sometimes the timber's been burned down to the
rock. You ought to see the miles of burnt timber
along the tracks, miles of bare gray trunks baking
in the sun. They say it gets absolutely different
down by the north shore where you're going." In
that country it got very hot at noontime, he said,
and very cool at night. Heavy blankets were necessary for the night. The nights are so awfully clear
you seem to be walking dreadfully close to the stars
and the way the northern lights keep swinging,
there's a kind of steady illumination. Peter listened,
asked questions, nodded, and the men beside them,
who were trying to concentrate on the wrestlers,
yelled at them to keep quiet. Hubert went on talking: it was a very blue country, the wooded hills
at noon time and the great lake always looked wonderfully blue. Small islands along the shore were
often just great bare slabs of rock rising smoothly
out of the water. All along the shore there would
be, no doubt, cool, measureless cliffs, and on the
summits, so high from the water that great trees

looked like bits of shrubbery, there would be almost impenetrable bush. Heavy leather shoes and a leather jacket would be needed if you went pushing your way through the bush. "Wait till the men up in that country see Marion," Hubert said. "They'll gawk at her for a week because they hardly ever see a woman like her." It would be necessary for them to watch the lake, for it was treacherous and rough and cold, and there were always wrecks in the stormy seasons, though for two summer months the water was warm. Peter said, "I'll bet there are trout streams up there that haven't been touched, but Marion will probably want to troll on the lake." They wondered whether it would be better to go all the way up by train, and make their way down to the lake, or go from the Sault by boat to the dock by the mouth of the Michipicoten, the wide green river. There was no use looking on the maps for the Mission. It wasn't marked. Peter went on planning till his voice was drowned by the roaring of the crowd. A two-hundred-and-fifty-pound Swede was throwing a three-hundred-pound Pole with a series of flying tackles, the Swede's great glistening body hurtling through the air and his clipped head striking the Pole, who expired slowly with terrible groans of agony and as much belching as he thought ought to accompany his humiliation. The brothers booed loudly. Then it was time for Peter to leave, and they left the Arena.

They parted on the corner by the gasoline station

near Peter's apartment house, which was brightly
lighted by rows of incandescent bulbs glowing on the
red-tiled roof of the station.

"Here's the key, kid," Peter said. "There's a quart
of whiskey in the drawer."

"I don't want to crack it alone. If Izzy isn't in,
do you mind if I take a bath in your place?"

"Not at all, please go ahead."

"I like the bath in your place. I like all the tiles."

"Why don't you get Izzy to make you some
coffee?"

"Do you think he would? He makes elegant
coffee. Is your banjo there?"

"The banjo's in the clothes closet. So long, kid."

"So long, boy. Tell your girl how I love her."

The big round white globes on top of the four
red pumps threw a soft, frosted light which shone
on the blue gas sparkling and bubbling as it was
pumped into the glass tube. Peter, walking along,
thought of a conversation he had had that afternoon with a doctor, a hurried man, who wanted to
write in his spare time a romantic poem that would
be a symbol of North American experience. Peter's
imagination was stimulated by his happiness. "I'll
think of an idea for the doctor," he thought. And he
thought of a massive, bronzed woman standing on a
hill looking out over a darkened field, listening for
sounds from the battle: she heard the sound of flying hoofs, and the strange animal, the terrible horse,
bearing a rider in shining armor, swept by, and she

knew the field was soaked with the blood of her race. When the newcomers from the far-away world came rushing over the hill, she knew they would rape her, so she tried to send her soul after the horse, for it was so swift in its passing and its hoofbeats were still pounding in her ears. "That's just what the doctor ordered," Peter thought with pleasure, and he imagined he could hear the horse's hoofbeats just ahead, only the bronzed woman's face, when he tried to think of her again, always became Marion's face. Then, near the house, he saw Marion come out as though she had been waiting at the window, and he was so eager, he waved his arm. She was wearing a neat black sweater, fitting her snugly, and a long black skirt. Her thick, blonde hair seemed almost ashen in the moonlight. With a lazy smile, she said, "Come on around to the back of the house and we'll sit by the lilac tree and talk." He took hold of her hand and they went back to the bench by the lilacs. Wondering why he was content to be silent, he held her hand in his two hands. Her hand felt inert and cold. He glanced at her. Her thoughts seemed far away, though her smile was indolent.

"I figure," he said, "I can get away at the end of the week and we could be away at least three weeks."

"Is that what you figure?" she said.

"Sure, that's what I figure."

Feeling that she wasn't thinking of him at all,

he said awkwardly, "It's pleasant sitting here, don't you think?"

"Peter, I'm not going away with you," she said bluntly. "There's no use beating about the bush. I decided to tell you to-night."

"No. We're going away," he said, still in good humor. "And bring that sweater you've got on along with you. Wear it all the time. I like it."

"Peter, I'm not going away."

"You promised you would, Marion."

"I know, but I've thought it over and it isn't worth it," she said, pulling her hand away as he tried to hold it. Her face was white and her eyes so narrow, he thought she was going to hit him. The intensity of her sudden anger bewildered him. "I don't get what you're driving at," he said. "I mean I don't know what's got into you."

"I'll tell you, Peter. You had a hard time persuading me in the first place and now I see there would be no compensations and there would be nothing ahead. I've thought over what it might mean in happiness or a lack of happiness and it all . . . oh, the game isn't worth the candle."

"You mean I can't offer much happiness to you."

"That's about it, I suppose," she said coolly.

"Why don't you marry me, Marion?"

"No, thanks," she said, with such abrupt cynicism that he could not answer. As he leaned back, she knew she had hurt him; his head from that angle looked large and round and tapered down to his chin. Full of mild wonder, she stared at him as if she were apt to laugh out loud. But she had been so casual that he grew resentful; he wanted to take hold of her and shake her. "You're mad," he said.

"No, I'm not, Peter," she said, wrinkling the skin under her eyes. She grew almost innocent and began to frown, looking down at the ground without speaking. "I've thought things over," she said.

"Then you're not going away with me?"

"No."

"We don't love each other enough, I suppose," he said.

"Not enough for that."

"Don't you ever want to see me again?" he asked humbly.

"It all isn't worth it, don't you see, Peter," she said impatiently, as though he were a child. He couldn't answer her. There was a grotesque, faun-like mildness about him when somebody had hurt and destroyed his confidence. All the strong feelings surging within him became one steady feeling of boyish wonder.

"You're a savagely candid person," he said at last.

"No, I'm not. But now I ought to be. I ought to be so much more candid." Feeling her way, trying to grope for words and watch him at the same time, she said jerkily, "Mother would have been just the girl for you years ago, wouldn't she, Peter? She

wouldn't have thought twice about running up
north in the summer with you, would she? Why do
you want me to go with you? She couldn't very well
do anything like that now though. . . . But why
couldn't she?" Then she paused, tried desperately to
go on, wavered as she glanced at his angry face, and
wondered whether to burst out resolutely with the
words she was holding back. Her mouth trembled,
she sighed, then said with quick savage loyalty, "I
like my mother. There's nothing wrong with her.
Her life has been unhappy, that's all," and shaking
her head stubbornly, she would not go on talking.

"Marion. Talk to me. Tell me what you're thinking. Why don't you trust me?" he said.

"I don't want to go away with you. I won't ever
marry anybody," she said like a petulant child. Then
she rapped her knuckles on the bench, held her fist
with the other hand, and her eyes filled with tears.

"If you insist on talking about your mother, go
ahead, shoot the works," he said.

"No, I won't talk about her with you. That would
be unbearable," she said, now more stubborn and
loyal. "I'll say only this, it'll be better, so much
better, if we don't go away together. I feel that deep
inside me."

"Tell me how long you think you'll be content to
live alone."

"Till I die, I suppose," she said faintly.

"Till you die," he said bitterly. "And then what?
What will you do in your grave? Death will be a

dandy guy for a lover on a northern trip. So you want me to leave you?"

"Yes," she whispered.

"Forever?"

"Forever."

"You can't see yourself. You're going to cry."

"Promise me, promise me you won't coax me," she said, deathly pale in the moonlight.

She was afraid because he had begun to speak his full love of her so earnestly. "Please, please let me go on loving you," he said as she leaned away from him. He put his hands that had begun to tremble on her shoulders. Just once she dug her fingers into the flesh of his arm, holding on to him, then she muttered, "I must. . . . Oh, go away." And she swallowed hard. The thick lilac leaves were brushing against her neck. It was dark in the shadow by the bush but a little farther out on the lawn the clipped grass was smooth in the moonlight. The grass was damp with heavy dew. A light from an upstairs back window shone slanting down to the lawn, making it seem darker on the bench by the lilac tree. As Marion lay back, the moon shone on her closed eyes. Overhead, the lighted window was raised; a shadow was thrown across the lawn, and a voice, Mrs. Gibbons' voice, said sharply, "Did I hear you talking to some one, Marion? Who's there?"

"Peter, Mother," she said, self-possessed and calm again.

"Why don't you come in instead of sitting out there?" Mrs. Gibbons said with some irritation.

Marion stood up and said, "Come on, Peter, I'm going to leave you." She was smiling. "I promised to go over and see Mona Howard after I had seen you to-night," she said. "Why don't you go in and see mother?"

"I don't want to see your mother," he said, growing angry.

"Sure you do, and she'd like to see you. I know she would. Go on, Peter. And you might as well tell her the way it has become with us." Indolent now, she walked away, and looked back at him as though speaking about the most casual matter in the world. They were at the front of the house. "By-bye, Peter," she said miserably, going down the street. Once she turned and waved her arm to him. As he watched her slender silhouette passing under the street light, he wanted to run after her, but he was afraid to disturb any further a feeling too deep within her for him to understand.

Confused, he looked back at the house, then he walked in to speak to Mrs. Gibbons.

As soon as he saw her he said, "Hello, Mrs. Gibbons, did you want to speak to me?"

"Hello, Peter, I thought you were with Marion," she said. "Where did you come from?" She was surprised and a bit flustered because she was dressed so carelessly.

"Marion's gone off by herself," he said.

"And you're upset," she said in a kindly, motherly tone. "Did you have a quarrel?"

"I don't know what was the matter with her."

"Never mind. Don't bother telling me about it." But she mumbled to herself, "She quarrelled with you all right, I can see that." She began to try and tidy some loose strands of hair at her ears. The plain, loose-fitting brown dress she was wearing made her look shapeless and heavy. Smiling with coy embarrassment, she said, "Wait in the living-room just a moment, please, Peter," and a blush began to redden her neck and face.

He paced up and down the room, feeling more bitter and resentful. He stood still by the window pressing his forehead against the pane. But as soon as Mrs. Gibbons returned, out of breath from having brushed back her shiny black hair, reddened her lips and cheeks and changed her dress in a hurry, he couldn't help smiling, for he had always liked her vivacious determination never to grow old. She had changed her stockings, too, and in hurrying one of her garters had been neglected, for the stocking was twisted and loose at the ankle. She had to pause and take a deep breath, though she was eager to start talking.

His thoughts were still muddled, but he was anxious for sympathy, so he said, "Marion gets a bit difficult at times. But there won't be any further difficulty. She doesn't want to see me. We're through."

"Through," she whispered, almost to herself. Taking another deep breath, she said, "Do you mind, Peter?"

"Yes, I do."

"Very much?"

"Yes," he said, and he seemed tired.

"If she could be frank, if you could be frank. . . . I felt from the first that she didn't really love you. I felt it, I felt it, I felt it. It's a good thing she told you. Poor boy, you're irritated and wounded now, but you'll be reconciled to that. Just what did she say?" she asked, leaning forward.

"I didn't think it would matter that much to you," he said.

"It does. Come on, Peter, tell me about it. Rely on me completely," she said warmly.

"I don't think relying on anybody would do much good," he said. "It's up to Marion."

Without trying to understand her, he began to look mournful; his damp, fair hair was curling, and his wide-open blue eyes were eager for sympathy. She began to fidget and her dark eyes grew soft and moist: it seemed to her that his usual solitary arrogance had been humbled, but for her, his drooping head and subdued eagerness still had majesty, as if he had wandered into far places and was now tired; and he seemed so marvelously like the young lover's image that had been in her head for years, she began to tremble. No longer petulant, she became shy and coaxing. "Forget her, do try and forget it, Peter," she whispered. "If it was a mistake . . . Peter, you ought to listen to me."

"Of course, I'm listening, Mrs. Gibbons," he said, for he had noticed that she was speaking with the nervousness of an older woman who trembles with helpless eagerness to please a young and selfish lover. Looking down, she noticed her loose stocking and, with deep embarrassment, she started tugging awkwardly at her skirt. This was the first time that they had not spoken to each other in a bantering tone. When he called at the house, she often made many absurd, motherly gestures, half good-natured, half serious, such as putting her arm around him and hugging him while protesting comically that she was an old woman. She had merely done a great many things mothers like to do with their daughters' husbands or sweethearts without having to think about it, but she had found in Peter some quality, the way he held his head, or his slender body, that revived all the passion of her young womanhood and reminded her of the only lover she had ever had, the young officer who had been killed at the war. She had come to believe that many of Peter's amusing gestures were those of her young and dead lover, and her secret passion for him became a renewal of the one true line of love in her life.

So she coaxed him: "You'll have to try and forget her. There'll be many other young fellows in her life. She's a very young woman. Oh, I know how wonderfully precious you'd be to me. I'd feel. . . ."

She was as nervous as a young girl with a most exacting lover. Her neck and face began to crimson as she moved over and sat beside him. Peter was not surprised when she put her arm around him, nor did he feel uneasy till her voice trembled, "I'll tell you how jealous I've often been of you," she whispered. "I've sometimes been so happy just thinking about you." While she was talking, her earnestness compelled his respect and sympathy. Her face, flushed, strong and handsome, had a very eager loveliness about it. Bending forward, she gave him a clumsy kiss full on the lips.

Just once he grinned with mischievious good humor, enjoying the depths of his own astonishment, then he was ashamed. Her timid smile wavered. Too humiliated to speak, she looked down again at her stocking which was gathered so loosely at the ankle.

With a wondering pity, he realized, somehow, that she was more than just a sensual, sentimental, middle-aged woman angling for a lover, and that her sincere feeling for him had been nourished by the strength and failure of her whole life. He tried to think of something to say. "Isn't there something I can do for you, Mrs. Gibbons?" he said.

"I don't know," she said.

While they were silent and she so shy and easy to hurt, he felt like a young man walking in a wood at night with a much older woman. They were sitting down close together. For some reason they both grew desperately shy. He could almost hear the older woman's heart beating with excitement. Her timid eagerness as she put out her hand and touched him made him fearful and ashamed. She looked so helpless, and they were both waiting. Nothing at all was said. Then he moved uneasily, looking away, and Mrs. Gibbons, so much older but now so much like a trembling young girl, knew at once with shame that he didn't love her.

"Isn't there something I can do for you, Mrs. Gibbons?" he repeated.

"No, nothing." She shook her head.

Gently he insisted, "Isn't there something . . . didn't we intend to discuss something?"

With her eyes startled and frightened, she looked up and said, "Did you hear some one coming in, Peter?"

"No. I didn't hear anything."

"I thought I heard the front door close and some one coming in."

"I didn't hear any one coming in."

She got up abruptly and walked over to the corner of the room to turn on the radio. As soon as her back was turned, Peter got up and hurried out to the front door. He was down the steps and near the sidewalk when he heard her calling from the door, "Peter," and her plump, well-manicured, soft white hands were up to her face as though she were crying out for something that had always eluded her.

Peter walked away, without looking back, and he felt with humility that there was nothing in his life to compensate Marion for anything she thought she might sacrifice: he only knew that he wanted her life to be entirely different from her mother's life. "Mrs. Gibbons became so soft and gentle. If she had only acted a bit different, if she had only acted like a lascivious old dame. But she wasn't like that at all. I couldn't say anything to her. There are some places where you can't go," he thought.

In his own room, in the house by the garage, he sat down on the bed and took off his shoes, then he opened his light blue shirt at the neck and pressed his lean face close to the mirror. His face looked solemn and white. He took a bottle of whiskey from the cupboard, poured himself a good four fingers, which he left neat and drank at once. But instead of feeling a glow of warmth, he only felt more subdued and alone, and he picked up his banjo, which his brother had left on the bed, and he strummed it once, looked at it, strummed it again and dropped it on the bed. For a long time he simply stared at the backs of two books on the shelf, a book by John Stewart Mill, the libertarian, and a book by Clarence Darrow, the American lawyer.

Then Hubert came into the room and smiled and said, "I was along the hall in Izzy's room. We heard you come in. He'll be in here any minute. Did you see your girl?"

"Yes."

"Have you got the date for the old nuptials fixed? When are you going away?"

"We're not going. We're breaking it."

"Why? What got into you?"

"It's her mother. Gee, Hubert, there's nothing to say." He smiled suddenly, then looked solemn just as suddenly, and then in a quick breathless rush of words told his brother about the conversation he had had with Marion and the conversation with her mother. "In a way it was like sitting beside a woman and watching the last warm bit of beauty in her life slipping away," he said.

"What did you do? What did you say?"

"Nothing. I think we both were sitting there wondering what was happening."

"It must have been ridiculous. The silly old dame. There ought to be a special saint to protect women of her age, don't you think? St. Mary of Egypt, or some one like that, Peter?"

"She didn't seem ridiculous. But there's no excuse for Marion," he added bitterly. "She needn't worry. She ought to have talked to me and been absolutely frank. There was nothing to be ashamed of. She needn't worry, I tell you. I'll not disturb her, do you hear? She can settle the whole matter with herself."

Then he saw Hubert looking round-eyed, resentful and very worried, so he said, "Don't be sentimental and silly about it, please," and he jumped up and said, "Here, come on, let's have a snort."

He filled the glasses. They sat up, faced each other and clicked their heels together and Hubert said politely, "Here's to you, Peter. Better times."

"Happy days, kid."

"Blood on the moon, Peter."

"No mud in our eyes."

They sat close together on the bed, both leaning forward as they looked solemnly at the door and waited for Isadore Klein to come in. Peter kept tugging at his nostrils with his right hand. Sometimes the brothers smiled weakly at each other.

Isadore Klein came into the room; he was a young Jew with an extraordinary appetite for food and girls who was being subsidized by some wealthy co-religionists to write a novel. Most of his money was spent before he got it, so he had to work three nights a week in a bakery. In his hand he was holding three manuscript pages he wanted to read to Peter. "Help yourself to the bottle, Izzy," Peter said. So Izzy sat down and went on talking about the bad winter that was ahead, and he thought the brothers were interested because they didn't answer, and then he paused, looked a bit disgusted and tried talking about a new German psychology. The brothers were looking down at the floor, and they seemed to be so close together and so far apart from him, he felt uncomfortable. "Do you think Dempsey can come back, Peter?" "No," Peter said. "I think he can if he'd get into condition," Izzy said, and waited, looking around. "Winston Churchill's

in the country talking about America and England,"
he said. "What do you think of Churchill?" "He's
obsolete. I don't think about the horse cars either,"
Peter said. "All right, don't get sore," Izzy said.
"He's no friend of mine. I'm a writer, not a politician." He went on talking steadily till Hubert
interrupted him unexpectedly by turning and asking
his brother if he had ever thought they both might
take a trip some time to Mexico and Yucatan to see
the Mayan ruins. Peter, looking more alert, turned
and listened to his brother respectfully. "Do you
guys know I've been talking to you for ten minutes?"
Isadore said. He glared at the brothers and walked
out of the room.

In a little while Peter said mildly to Hubert that
he had intended to show him a letter he got from
their father. "He's wondering if I'm getting along
quickly enough," Peter said. He suggested to his
brother that it would be a good idea if they both
wrote enthusiastic letters to their father; he would
write about important judges, bankers or clergymen
he might see or meet and Hubert could write about
places and things he had seen. "If he gets depressed,
he might have another apoplectic stroke," Peter
said.

But the following night while Peter was still
sullen from disappointment, he picked up Patricia
Lee, after sitting beside her in a show, a tall, slender, smooth blonde with an unsmiling face and a

wide, thin lower lip. She lived at the Windermere Hotel, close by the foreign section of the city, and he went home with her and they talked for many hours. At one time she had wanted to make hats and some day, maybe, own a millinery shop, but her fingers never seemed to get nimble enough. The first time she had been out of work, for nearly a year, she had had a very bad, unhappy time, with no place to sleep, and she had been arrested on a vagrancy charge and taken to the police station. After that, a deep fear was always inside her that she would have no money and would have to go on the streets and be arrested again. She had a notion in her head that if she always wore high-class clothes and looked cold, indifferent, aloof and independent, no one would ever interfere with her. Carefully she inquired whether Peter had a job and was willing to spend money on her. He stayed with her two days. Then he went to live with her.

5

MARION hardly tried to amuse herself. She preferred to be alone. If there had been a racing meet at the Woodbine she would have spent the afternoons at the track but the horses had long ago moved on to another city. Estaban, a five-to-one shot, ran second and the Italian, Badame, phoned her. All the time she felt very calm, very still, waiting and really playing a game with herself, pretending she could secretly be constant to her own love for Peter. In the afternoons she lay in the hammock in the shade on the north side of the house, reading, and sometimes dreaming of the blue Algoma Hills. At one time she had thought of being with Peter in the immense solitude of that country; only a little while ago she had thought of them being at the foot of the waterfall on the Magpie River, or trolling for fish in a gray misty morning when the water was very still on the great inland sea; or pushing their way through thick, sweet-smelling underbrush, following a trail only a foot wide and sitting down to rest by a patch of sunlight near a trout pool where they could relax lazily and try a million new ways of love-making. But now she found a melancholy pleasure in dreaming of herself alone, high and solitary, drifting among great cones of pines in deep valleys in the solitude of wooded hills. Even thinking of living in the unbroken peacefulness of days at the clean white-washed boarding house at the Mission delighted her. There was one small sun-baked beach on the black rocky shore, far lovelier in the moonlight than all the hills and overhanging rain-washed cliffs. She amused herself thinking she might still go to this country; some of its solitary steadiness was in her now, she felt. And while lying in the hammock on the veranda, she noticed that the grass was very long on the lawn in front of the old house next door. By the unpainted lattice work at the base of the veranda there had been a flower bed, and even now a few brown, withered, rotting stalks stuck up out of the dark earth. On the thick green grass was one yellow, square blotch, matted down, just behind the big red and white "For Sale" sign. For days, when the grass was growing green, the heavy sign had been on that spot, blown down by the wind. "I wonder who put it up again," she thought.

Marion saw a vegetable wagon and a baker's wagon passing each other on the street. A foreigner, whose face was deeply creased from smiling, was on the vegetable wagon, beside him, a little kid in gray. The horse was skinny, with a deep hollow in its aged back; the sweating skin, drawn tightly across the jutting and angular hip bone, was polished in the sunlight. On the horse's head was a battered old straw sunshade, and its ears stuck out ridiculously. As the baker and vegetable man talked together, the baker offered a lemon pie for three oranges. Standing up, Marion called, "Toss me an orange, will you?" She took a nickel from her purse, as the Italian got down to the sidewalk, and flicking it with her thumb, sent it in a gleaming arc through the sunlight to the sidewalk. He picked it up. When he tossed the orange, Marion said to herself, "If I catch it, Peter will . . ." but the orange came too suddenly, hitting the arm of the chair, bounding over to her knee, and she caught it just as it dropped to the floor. So she was neither disappointed nor glad, just puzzled, and she smiled to the vegetable man, who waved back to her. Ever since she had been a little girl she had played such games of chance with herself.

As she laughed lazily she felt like having cheerful company, some one who would talk rapidly to her. She got up, rushed into the house and put on her smartest clothes, a long light-blue crepe dress, fitting her tightly at the waist and the hips, and a white panama hat with a plain blue band. Quite pleased with her appearance, she went to call on her friend, Mona Howard, and her baby.

Mona was a short, black-haired, vivacious young woman with eyes bright and round like polished shoe buttons. She had always been a tireless, gay girl, with so many wild ways that her father used to despair of her: she was a madcap at any roadhouse party; her gin and pajama parties were well known; and yet when she had married an engineer

with some money and had a baby, she surprised
everybody by being content. The baby seemed to
be her whole life. As soon as Mona saw Marion, she
hugged her warmly, then pushed her back at arm's
length till she could have a better look at her.
Again she kissed her on each cheek and said, "You
darling, you're so stunning and so cool looking."
She was just as excitable and eager as Marion was
cool and composed, but they had been friends for
years. With her arm around Marion, she hurried her
upstairs to see the baby.

She put the baby on a pillow and they both stood
back and tried to get it to smile at them as Mona
explained that in the first place at the hospital they
had thought a cæsarian operation would be necessary. The remarkable part of it all was that just
two years ago, two doctors had assured her that she
would not have a baby. Marion couldn't resist
stooping and brushing her cheek against the down
on the small head so like a doll's head with the
round violet eyes. Timid, she asked Mona if she
could pick it up, and Mona rather reluctantly con-
sented. She held it close to her. For some reason,
as she held it against her body and felt the life in
it, she was startled to think, with a catch in her
breath, that she probably would never have a baby
of her own. And as she held it much closer to her,
her lower lip moved faintly and her blue eyes were
moist.

Mona, glancing at her, said, "Why, Marion, I had

no idea you were so fond of children. You ought
to have one."

"I had no idea myself," she said.

"You ought to get married at once. You have no
idea what fun a baby is. Marry Peter Gould."

"But why Peter?"

"Go on now. Everybody knows how fond you are
of Peter."

"But he has no money at all, and, oh, it wouldn't
occur to either one of us," she said, trying to conceal
how flustered she was as she smiled and looked
away evasively.

6

PETER was living at his hotel as if nothing disturbing had happened except perhaps that his brother didn't come to see him. He wrote regularly to his father; it was always in his mind that he looked like his father. Occasionally he had lunch with the hurried doctor who wanted to write epic poems about America. He did not let himself think of Marion, though sometimes, when he was reading law, he thought of the journey north they had planned; it seemed to be something apart from both of them glimpsed for one brief moment when fate had held it out. Such a journey became something to marvel at without any bitterness. He had some newspaper friends whom he used to see when he dropped into the city hall press gallery. Straddling a chair and tilting forward with his hat far back on his head, he would watch the fellows playing poker, with a serene smile on his face. It was hard to say whether he was extremely interested in the game or utterly indifferent, but once he interrupted the play to ask Bill McLaughlin, a red-faced, curly-headed court reporter who was a fanatical fisherman, what he knew about the salmon-bellied trout in Lake Superior. McLaughlin began to talk about the fishing villages and the black flies in the bush that came down to the shore line, till the newspapermen he was playing with objected angrily to his interrupting the game. "I don't know why," McLaughlin said apologetically, "but that guy's got the Algoma shore country on the brain." Peter grinned and lied, "I was up there once when I was a kid." No one doubted him because he had the look in his eyes of a man who was trying to remember half-forgotten, far-away things; it was as though some one had waved a wand in front of him and showed him where the journey might have led. In his pocket he had two railroad maps marking the route to the Algoma Hills, and showing where the lake boats touched the mainland. He had persisted further and found out how far north along the shore the gravel road extended before ending in rock and timber. He had found out that there was an Ojibway Indian reserve far along the shore from the river and the Mission. It was much harder to find out how long the French people had been at the Mission, for no one knew, and no books told about them. He read about the gold mines of the country that had been wildcatted, and the vast iron ore deposits; and without ever having seen it, he could talk glibly about the blue lake teeming with whitefish and lake trout, and of the abundance of pickerel at the river mouths. He had found out all these things like a man who learns about the things he expects to encounter if he should ever have the good fortune to make a long-postponed journey.

After the short, heavy thunderstorm on the hot-

test afternoon all summer, Peter was walking down
the city hall steps with Alderman Redpath. A
divinely happy smile lit up his face and his large
head was held, quizzical, and birdlike, on one side as
though he were still full of wonder at something
that had delighted him. He was wearing a loose,
baggy, gray tweed suit. He looked untidy except
for a soft, almost white, expensive felt hat the
woman he lived with had coaxed him to buy. Beside
him, with a sour expression, and a gates-ajar collar,
walked the alderman who was supposed to be one
of Mrs. Gibbons' most devoted admirers and who
was so successful as a politician that young lawyers
followed his taste in hats, collars, clothes and ties.
Peter and the alderman were coming from the courts
where they had opposed each other in a small piece
of litigation. As they walked down the stone steps
in the sunlight and then parted, Peter saw his
brother waiting for him by the cenotaph.

"Camerado," he called. "I salute you. Have I
kept you waiting?"

"Not at all, Citizen Gould. Who am I to com-
plain when you've been in such distinguished company?"

"Bless the dear alderman. Take a look at him
swaggering along there. He gets so puffy and
swollen with his own eloquence from day to day he'll
soon float off, eh?"

Linking arms and chuckling to themselves they
went down the steps past the cenotaph where

pigeons were resting and where flowers and floral wreaths heaped at the base now withered in the sun. After the shower the sun glistened on vertical, white, skyscraper surfaces down the street. Speaking with apologetic diffidence, Peter said, "Come on home and have dinner with us. It won't kill you, Hubert."

"No. I'd like to, but that girl and I get into each other's hair. In the first place it was different. You had the blues and were impulsive enough to want to keep her. But now, honestly, I can't bear to see you being so stubborn and willful about trying to hurt yourself. You're going around like a man stumbling over his own shadow. The other night I talked to you for an hour and you hardly answered me. What am I to say?"

"I say you're kidding me."

"No. It was the night we were drinking at Mrs. Goldstein's. I was trying to tell you that the ancient Egyptians must have been marvelous, and when you looked blank I switched to some mighty interesting economic predictions, and you suddenly grinned and asked me if I had made any plans for a trip to Mexico."

"I've become reticent, that's all. I'm going native. Nobody talks these days anyway, so I just grunt."

"Peter, listen to me. If you can't get Marion off your mind, go and see her."

"That shower simply made it hotter. My clothes are sticking to me." Peter half closed his eyes in the sunlight and said, smiling, "What'll you say if I marry Patricia?"

"I'll say in that case that you're getting pretty tiresome. She's a fine big strapping wench but. . . ."

"Listen, Hubert," Peter said irritably. "It might be a good thing. Can't you see I ought to start everything all over again? It would be better to start with a girl like Pat because it makes the renunciation of everything I wanted before more complete. You think my taste is pretty low. All right, it ought to be low to start with so I could work my way up to a new kind of dignity." He went on talking but his words began to get mixed up. His thoughts began to confuse him and he seemed upset. "What's the use of talking about it?" he said. "I'll see you to-night. I'll meet you at Bowles' at a quarter after ten and we'll have a game of billiards. That's the main thing, eh, camerado? So long." With an independent shrug of his shoulders he walked away as if he had just found a marvelous interest in a new, quiet life. Hubert had so much to say to him that he could only shake his head and remain inarticulate while the sun shone on his brother's light felt hat and on the back of his neck as he turned the corner.

Peter, walking aimlessly, was passing the department store windows, which were a whole block long, and in every window were tall figures with lovely silver heads and aristocratic profiles displaying many colored new fall costumes for women. There were

plain woollen dresses and neat brown suits with
slender lines. There was one particular tight-fitting
red woollen dress on a silver-faced figure. For a
long time Peter looked at it with his face pressed
against the plate glass. A far-away look was in
his eyes as if he wasn't actually seeing the dress
at all. "Probably in September, by the middle of
the month, Marion would be wearing a dress like
that. I can just see her hurrying along the street
with it fitting her like a glove. Of course she would
wear it with the cool stylishness of the silver man-
nequin," he thought. Full of a kind of childish pleasure he moved slowly from one big window to another, looking eagerly at all the new costumes,
selecting only the most distinctive ones for Marion.
As he decided definitely that a certain fall coat
would please her, she became so real in his thought,
he could almost put out his hand and touch her.
In the next window there were evening dresses with
satin shoes, a whole window of shoes with one dainty
pair of red satin slippers close to the plate glass in
the corner. He stared solemnly at this one pair of
little red slippers and felt impatient with subdued
excitement. "I'd give anything in the world just to
see that pair of slippers on her feet," he said. "If
I could just see them on her feet, maybe when she
was standing waiting for somebody." As he crossed
the street, still walking slowly, he thought, "I'd
want Marion to remain exactly as she is. I wouldn't
want any part of her to change. Why did I use to

argue with her about anything?" One night she had begun to cry because he had insisted she ought to like a book by D. H. Lawrence which had appealed to him.

He was on his way to the Windermere Hotel, going up Spadina, the wide street running through the garment-making centre of the city. Garment workers on strike had gathered outside one of the buildings. Policemen on horses were holding the crowd back. Puddles of water were still on the pavement; great light blotches had dried after the rain, but the sun still glistened on pools of water. The horses were held back on their hind legs, their glistening brown bodies poised with the front legs pawing at the crowd. "If I stay looking at it, I'll want to get into it," he thought. "I can watch it from the hotel window."

At the hotel desk the manager with the small hands and the enormous fat neck beamed when he saw Peter coming in, and the henna-haired girl at the switchboard looked at him wistfully as if she would like to have a lover, but Peter went right upstairs to his room. It was a large room covered with old green carpet. By the white mantel was Peter's banjo, which he never used now. A big, handsome, fair-skinned woman, wearing a pink negligée, was sitting in the one deep comfortable chair, and on the carpet beside her was a pair of pink mules, three motion-picture magazines she had borrowed from the girl at the desk downstairs, an ash tray, quite empty but like an island in the sea of ashes around it, and a box of stuffed figs. With a cool, lazy smile Patricia curled her legs up under her and stretched luxuriously like a sleek cat, but when she noticed that Peter's eyes had the dreamy expression in them which always made her feel uncomfortable, she jumped out of the chair, rushed across the room in her stockinged feet and threw her arms around him. "Peter, Peter, pumpkin eater, here's your girl, your pumpkin, Peter, aren't you going to eat her? I've been waiting and waiting. Aren't you going to hug me, aren't you going to hug me? That's the boy. Say, Peter, did you remember to bring the salted almonds and the cheese?"

"I'm stupid, Pat. Mind you, I forgot all about it."

"What's the matter, boy? You look done to a turn. Don't I make you feel better? I'm not getting on your nerves again, am I?"

"Don't keep rubbing that in. Just because I threw a fit of temper the other night and made you miserable, you've had the willies ever since."

"I was upset because you're always so sweet to me. You are a sweet boy, Peter. I feel so happy when you're feeling good and seem to like me. Don't you want to have people in to-night?"

"Sure I do. Go ahead."

"I don't want to, you know, Peter, if you don't. I just want to know if you feel sociable. Sometimes you seem to like people and then you're swell and

everybody likes you. You were grand that night
when you told all those French Canadian stories. I
could never get that dialect, 'lack zis, lack zat,
comme ci, comme, ça.' How's that?"

"O. K. I'll bet the Lord intended you for musical
comedy."

"Or burlesque, I'll bet, with other big girls in the
back row," she said.

Peter took a case book on contract law from his
brief bag and sat down by the window to read cases
that he ought to have read in the office: during
the last few days he had made little progress at the
office; the days had been hot, anyway, and it was
easy to plan to work at night in the hotel. And
now he rested the book on his knee and then looked
out the window and down at the crowd that had
grown larger. Some one had thrown a brick. A blue
wedge of cops charged swinging their batons, bowl-
ing over any one in the way. The crowd was driven
back slowly. Then Peter turned and smiled good-
naturedly at Patricia. He looked down at his shoes.
"I ought to have got a shoe shine," he thought, but
he was wondering why it was that he felt so close
to Patricia and so much at peace with her in that
one room. She was looking over at him shyly as
though feeling that if he weren't satisfied with her
she would lose the security she had in her life with
him. Her shy glance seemed to awaken him, and he
understood all of a sudden why they, who remained
strangers in so many ways, wanted to go on living

together in the room with the green carpet and the sagging chairs. For years she had been kept by men who, in the long run, ill treated her and then got rid of her. She was sitting there, fretting, because she knew that something was worrying him. Even the massiveness of her figure seemed to make her all the more mute. If Peter should say he was tired of her, there was nothing ahead but months of tramping the streets, trying to hold a job when God, Himself, seemed to have intended that she lose it. But now, as he glanced at her, he was full of sympathy, for the uneasiness that was so deep in her life and in her soul seemed but a part of the vast discontent and unrest in his own soul, and on this afternoon, at least, it was as though they were being driven closer together by the force of the agitation that was all around them and within them, too. "Like two strangers, we huddle together for warmth on a winter night," he thought, and he smiled with surprising warmth. Then he turned and looked out the window again; he was looking over the roofs of the houses, over the tops of trees and the electric wires still wet and glistening from pole to pole, at one small city sparrow fluttering around a chimney that stuck up against a white cloud. And the mood which was half hidden within him but never transient deepened and he had a picture in his head of Marion walking ahead of him out of the station; his eyes had followed the slight rhythmic sway of her hips moving in an arc as the shaft of sunlight struck the back of her neck.

Patricia startled him by saying quite loudly, "What are you thinking about, Peter, boy? I was looking at the riot before you came in. You don't want to get interested in that. Stay out of it, that's what I say. I just want to be left alone myself. My father was a cop. He taught me that."

"I wasn't looking at anything," he said. "Right now, out there on the street, a fellow got away from a cop and climbed a telegraph pole and the cop went up after him. Just opposite the window there's a sparrow perched on a telegraph wire. How does the bird know how to avoid the live wires so it won't get killed? For some reason it makes me think of the country. I had intended to go away this summer."

"Were you going away with a girl?"

"Yes."

"Did you love her very much?"

"Very much."

"Was she like me? Just a bit like me in some way?"

"No, hardly at all. You're a much bigger girl."

Patricia, for some reason, looked sullen and hurt. She muttered, "Oh, I wasn't suggesting that I was like her. I wouldn't suggest such a thing as that, Mr. Gould. Pardon me, pardon me."

Peter, laughing good-naturedly, went over and

put his arm around her as if he were willing to worship her, and when she sighed, and smiled, he said, "You won't mind if I leave here at a little after ten to-night, will you?"

"To go where? To go and meet your other girl, I bet."

"To go and meet my brother. I haven't got any other girl."

"I don't like your brother. I think he talks about me. These smug, smiling-faced boys who aren't interested in parties or girls, or hardly anything but just their brothers, they give me a pain."

"He doesn't like you either."

"I don't care. Peter, take me out to eat early. I'm tired sitting here. Let's go right now."

"What would you like to eat? Look, I've got two dollars."

"I'd like oysters on the half shell. Wouldn't you love oysters with tomato sauce if we could get them? I wonder if we could get oysters."

"There's no R in August. You'll have to wait a month," he said.

She put on her plain, good-looking felt hat and her light coat with the clean lines and the scarf knotted at the neck so it would blow over her shoulder, and when she looked in the mirror, she was so childishly pleased, she put her hand on her hip and smiled openly. Whenever she was sure she was well dressed, even her disposition seemed to change; she became confident, cool and even a little arrogant.

Her face was tinted with a tan powder which, with her fair hair and her brown eyes, made her look all golden and massive. Peter laughed and liked her. He began to amuse her with bits of gay conversation turned so neatly that the words delighted her.

They were good-humored and gay with each other long after they returned to the hotel, but when the company arrived Peter's gayety passed far beyond Patricia's control. There were three girls, who were friends of Patricia, and three fellows, one of whom was a sallow-faced medical interne, an old friend of Peter's. After Peter had had a few drinks he began to entertain the company with a whole series of pantomimes and everybody rocked with laughter at his foolish antics. Patricia laughed too, and was very proud of him, but, like a nervous mother, she was uncertain of what he might do. All of a sudden his good humor passed away. White-faced, he sat on the edge of the chair as though wondering how he might humiliate himself. Without any warning, he stood up, pulled off his coat and shirt and walked around, naked down to the waist. They laughed but he was utterly indifferent to the laughter. Then he grew sullen. His own friend, the medical interne, was watching him with his eyes half closed and a slight smile on his face. As Peter passed by him, he whispered, "You're punch drunk, Peter." "Eh?" Peter said. "What's the matter?" the doctor said. "Did your girl blow away? You can't take it on the chin, eh?" Peter looked at him with blank blue eyes, and then he suddenly picked up a glass of beer and threw it in his friend's face. As soon as he did it he became like a shy and humiliated boy; he pleaded to be pardoned; he offered to try and stand on his head in front of the medical interne, who only smiled.

Then he felt quite sober and he took his hat and left the hotel. Outside, he stood on the wide street by the hotel entrance, feeling the light breeze coming up from the lake. He looked up at the lighted window of the room with the green carpet. They were still laughing, the laughter floating down. Relief at being alone and outside surged within him. He walked away to meet his brother. There seemed to be so many things he wanted to say that he began to hurry.

7

PETER met his brother and they had a game of billiards in the pool parlor over Bowles' lunch room. Neither of them played billiards very well but they treated each other's game with the respect that one master owes to another. Then they went out to the street, stood together silently looking up at the city hall clock, and as if they knew exactly what they intended to do, they started to walk, falling into step at once. Peter began to make a conversation about the possibility of a war in China: he had the greatest admiration for the Chinese, he said, but of course, Hubert seemed to know that Peter was saying none of the things he had intended to say. Hubert began to ask a few questions, when Peter, for no reason, switched the conversation and began to talk rapidly about the new revolutionary spirit, wondering if it meant the decline of the old Western world. He himself intended to be utterly and newly nihilistic, he said and, pushing his brother away playfully, he began to chuckle to himself. Hubert was eager to have his brother go on talking, as though he thought him a leader, or at least some one who would approach everything differently, but Peter, looking up suddenly, recognized the young priest who was passing by, Father Vincent Sullivan, from the Cathedral. "Good-evening, Father," he said, raising his hat. Startled, the priest said gravely, "Good-evening," and passed by. He crossed over to the other side of the road, solitary and hurrying, neat, clean, and freshly shaven, the shiny top of his hard straw hat glinting under the street light.

"Do you know him, Peter?"

"Hardly. I just met him once at Mrs. Gibbons' place. He called to see her but she was out, and he didn't stay to talk to Marion. He's shy."

"Look at him hurrying along there, hardly looking to the right or left, with his rosy cheeks and his red lips and the hat sitting squarely on the top of his head."

"I like him. Wouldn't it disturb him, though, trying to give spiritual consolation to Mrs. Gibbons? Imagine."

"He's green all right, if that's what you mean."

"No. I mean how could he sympathize with her and understand her unless he knew what was behind her whole life. I don't. She's mixed up and easy to misunderstand." Growing hesitant, he said, "The other day I saw Marion and her mother downtown crossing the street together. She had hold of her mother's arm. They seemed very friendly."

"Why didn't you speak to them? Did they see you?"

"They didn't see me." Then he added quietly, "Mrs. Gibbons has been writing letters to me. I haven't answered them. I can't figure out what she wants. She says she wants to speak to me again. It's a tough job trying to figure her out. She really is such a fine style of a woman in one way. She ought to be such a proud big-feeling woman."

As Peter stopped abruptly, Hubert felt he was forcing him to make a conversation about matters he had tried to avoid. They were walking down by the waterfront and along by the piers. As they stood by the rail, looking down at the dark water, at the small waves bobbing and splashing faintly, the little sticks on water being tossed up against the pier, tossed back again and coming back with every lapping wave, Peter, finding words with difficulty, said he really believed Marion thought she would be happier without him. She had tried to destroy his good happy feeling for everybody, he said. Then he was silent again, looking over beyond the dark warehouses and across the flat, barren sandy stretch of reclaimed land as far as the new grain elevators, white, round, clean and solid in the moonlight as if they had just been polished and set down there in the level wasteland. Suddenly he began to talk about Marion; he made no effort at all to check the flow of words that poured out of him. There was no sequence or point in anything he was saying except that he was remembering things about her; whenever they were downtown together in the evenings they used to stand on the scales outside the drug-store and get weighed; she weighed one hundred and eighteen pounds, usually, though last summer she went as high as one hundred and twenty-three; her high-heeled shoes used to hurt her instep when they walked too far, so she had got a special pair of short-heeled, soft, blue kid shoes. He went on talking away like this till he was exhausted, then he had nothing to say at all.

As the brothers turned to walk back uptown, they felt much closer together, as if somehow the full intimacy of their comradeship had been restored. When they passed under the street light they were both leaning forward a little, walking in step, their arms linked. They went over to Mrs. Finklestein's to have some beer. Feeling sociable and eager, they put on several pantomimes for the amusement of the customers, laughed their heads off, told the most preposterous lies to Mrs. Finklestein, and had a hard time persuading the other patrons that they finally had to be leaving.

But when Peter returned to the Windermere Hotel, he felt tired and short-tempered. Patricia, who was lying down on the sofa, half dressed, pouted because he had been away so long and said, "Oh, I say, you don't mind leaving a fellow alone, do you?"

"Have you been alone long?"

"Have I? Why I thought I'd go blotto unless you came in," she said, using an English sporting accent she often affected when wearing certain clothes.

"Never mind the accent, Pat," he said. "It

doesn't sound good to-night." But she was too lazy
to defend herself. She smiled, then yawned and half
closed her eyes.

That night he could not sleep. Outside a night-
hawk was screeching and swooping over the low
roofs. He started thinking how Mrs. Gibbons as an
eager young woman must have stumbled blindly
against a barrier that was too high for her to climb,
so she had to fret and wait and wonder what was
on the other side. Perhaps there was always a clear
sunlit field on the other side. The window drapes
swayed sensuously in the street breeze. He suddenly asked himself what the journey north with
Marion might have led to, wondering if there was
some meaning behind it he could not understand: he
tried to ponder the meaning of its magic as though
he were close to an explanation that could be grasped
intuitively; only it was like staring till your eye
ached at the brilliant white peak of a mountain that
could not quite be seen. "It's something apart from
me that I've built up till I can see it concretely, yet
it's something growing bigger within me, like an
ache or a final necessity," he thought. "Why should
I do without thinking about it? I can't help wishing we had gone up there." He could no more do
without wishing, or feeling the hurt that went
with wishing, than an early Christian in a period
of dreadful spiritual dryness could do without
longing for God. He started to mutter as a child
going to sleep mutters a rhyme, "Marion, clarion,

darion, Darien, the peaks of Darien, silent upon a peak in Darien." Then he opened his eyes and saw a white shape of her fading into the corners of the room. He saw her smooth, rounded arm disappearing in the dark wall shadows. Tossing in bed, he blamed it on the beer he had been drinking, but then he muttered, "Marion, come into the room, come in through the window. Put your head on the pillow. I'm terribly in love with you." He tried to be still by holding his body stiff, but when he closed his eyes, some part of her was shining everywhere in the room. He kept on tossing with longing, and thrust his bare foot out above the bed covers. Moonlight, streaming in from the window, shone on the sole of his foot as the night bird kept on screeching and swooping over the low roofs.

8

AFTER eating a heavy meal in the evening, Mrs. Gibbons said to Marion, "I'm a weak old woman. I don't imagine I've got more than two or three years to live, I mean really live. Then I'll be like any other old woman. I want to die before that."

It was the first time in days she had talked about herself. Usually they talked about such matters as what they would like to have for dinner, or whether the little plumed, black, felt hat, dipping down over one eye, and displayed in all the store windows, would remain in fashion long. In being so casual, they were really feeling their way slowly toward each other.

"Why, Mother," Marion said, "you ought to be looking forward to the most restful period of your life."

"With what? With whom? What comfort is there for me in growing old? Who is to grow old with me? I'm left alone. I'm utterly without any one."

"Perhaps you and father. . . ."

"Tush, tush. Mark my words. We'll not hear from him again. He's gone for good, but do you know, it makes me feel all the more alone, now he's gone."

But right after dinner Mrs. Gibbons was lively again, dressed in black velvet cut very low to show the curve of her ample breast, of which she was very

proud because of its whiteness and firmness. Early
in the evening, at twilight, Alderman James Redpath, the lawyer, called to see her. For a few moments, waiting for Mrs. Gibbons, he talked with
Marion and smiled boldly. At first Marion was
going to ask him if he had seen Peter, but she took
a dislike to his bulging blue eyes and his fair hair
and felt at once that a bulldozing manner was underneath his too affable graciousness. In the courts, his
favorite method of cross-examination was to toss
cheap wisecracks at a witness who was unable to
retaliate. As he talked to Marion, and liked her
deep husky voice, her blonde head and her lazy assurance, he tried to interest her as a man of affairs, a
man who knew everybody, belonged to all the lodges
and was one of the noisiest aldermen in the council.
He talked, grinning, his blue eyes staring, in a just-
between-you-and-me manner. Mrs. Gibbons, who
had taken an interest in him, had advanced him
money for his last election, so he called as often
as possible to express his gratitude to his lovely
benefactress.

Marion left him when her mother came into the
room. He said to Mrs. Gibbons, and loud enough, of
course, for Marion to hear, "What a great pleasure
indeed to meet your daughter. What a dandy girl!"

Marion, who was listening, thought despondently,
"Surely I won't be receiving men like that when I'm
mother's age." Full of pity for her mother, she
wanted to go back to the room, very tenderly put

her arm around her, and tell Redpath never to come to the house again. "Mother, if you could only love me more. Or if I were more gentle with you, would you have to bother with men like that?" she thought, as she put her hand up to her lips, listening.

Mrs. Gibbons, for some reason, lost all her vivacious good humor quickly. Redpath, who was disappointed, did not stay more than half an hour. Mrs. Gibbons, looking sedate and subdued, spoke quietly to Ag and went out, walking along the street by herself. As soon as she had gone Marion said to Ag, "Where has my mother gone, do you know?"

"She's gone down to the Cathedral."

"What for?"

"I don't know."

Marion smiled but found herself thinking of the way her mother had talked at dinner time, and how she had been filled with unhappiness, as though feeling the last of her youth slipping away from her. There were times when Marion was both amused and puzzled by her mother's idle fancies, and she could never really decide whether she was extraordinarily sincere, or unbelievably deceitful.

Yielding to a sudden curiosity, Marion put on her light coat with the belt at the waist, in case it should get chilly, and walked a few blocks south toward the Cathedral. It was twilight and she was going down the street with a long stride, her hands deep in her pockets, her fair hair combed loosely, falling back behind her small ears, for she had not bothered to wear a hat. The neighborhood changed rapidly as she got closer to the Cathedral, which was high and splendid though surrounded by squat rooming houses and small factories. Its spire stuck up darkly against the light sky. Marion sauntered through the gates and up the walk to the heavy doors, her hands still in her pockets, a cool, tall, rather large-boned girl with an imperturbable head. At this moment, Father V. Sullivan, the youngest priest at the Cathedral, was just coming out of the vestry. He glanced at her and recognized her. This reserved, serious, good-looking young fellow, seemed rather surprised to see her, for though he had the greatest admiration for Mrs. Gibbons, he knew her daughter had drifted away from the Church; possibly, he sometimes thought, because of the influence of her irreligious father. As he noticed her careless way of wearing her clothes and her uncovered head, he was disturbed to think of wantonness. "Why do I have to think of that?" he thought as he raised his hat. He wanted to stop and be cheerful, but she hardly even smiled politely. She looked like such an independent and aloof young woman that he hesitated to speak, but he said, "Good-evening, Miss Gibbons."

"Good-evening, Father Sullivan."

"It's a lovely evening, isn't it? I suppose you're waiting for your mother?"

"Yes, Father."

"You've been away, I hear. We must see more of you now."

"How did you know I was away, or back?"

"Oh, we hear everything, you know," he said, smiling and passing on.

She did not go into the Cathedral, for her head was uncovered, but she pushed open one of the inner doors. Inside the church it was dimly lighted. In the last pew by the door was an old man with his thin hands clenched desperately and his bony head drooping. A priest was hearing confessions, and on the bench by the confessional a few people were waiting. Marion saw her mother over to one side, up toward the front, close by the altar of the Blessed Virgin. She had expected to see her mother praying with some of the dignity of a prominent lady of the parish; instead she saw a heavy woman with bowed head, whose eyes were never raised, whose self-consciousness had been utterly destroyed in her prayer of humble adoration. Marion waited, and at last she saw her mother coming down the aisle with bowed head to sit on the penitents' bench at the confessional by the old man with the bony head. Then the old man went into the confessional. Mrs. Gibbons waited, telling her beads. Her lips moved in prayer. But when the old man pushed aside the thick curtains and came out of the confessional Mrs. Gibbons was startled, for it was her turn to go in. Getting up clumsily, she moved back to the pews as though she had decided at the last moment that she couldn't go to confession.

Marion turned away, feeling a little ashamed of

herself for having intruded into this quiet hour in
her mother's life. She went out hastily. It was quite
dark. As she walked back home she was bewildered
by the curious contradictions in her mother's character. She was disturbed, feeling that somehow all
her own notions had been upset. How could a
woman like her mother pray with so much honest
devotion, she asked herself, and be neither honest
nor dishonest? Nothing was plain, nothing very
simple, nothing could be stated in just so many
words, and so everything was all mixed up. But she
began to feel a new, warm sympathy for her mother.

After she got home, she heard her mother downstairs in the library at the front of the house, and
she hurried down to speak to her, intending to be
gentle and agreeable, but just as she went into the
room, she saw her writing an address on an envelope.
Her mother still had her coat and hat on as if intending to go out at once. There was no doubt about it,
the letter was addressed to Peter. Concealing the
letter, and looking covertly at Marion, Mrs. Gibbons
went out on her way down to the letterbox at the
corner.

In a mild manner, Marion assured herself her
mother was writing to Peter about business matters.
"I won't think about it at all," she thought; but as
she went out of the room, going upstairs, she looked
like a big, angry, desperate girl with very cold steady
eyes, for she was stunned by the confusion in her
thoughts, and her feeling of absolute hatred toward

her mother. "She's spoiled things enough for me," she said, sitting down in the darkness by the window in her own room. "I'll fix her." Steadily, she became more angry: she held her fists against her breast. "I'll hurt her," she said. "She can suffer till she's black and blue." And she trembled and closed her eyes and felt dizzy with the strength of her anger. She waited, alert, and the air in the room seemed to press hotly against her temples. Every noise in the house was plain. Her mother came in, closed the front door and came upstairs at once to her own room. On the street corner, under the light which Marion could see from the window, a fellow and a girl stopped, and the fellow, pushing his hat far back on his head, began talking earnestly. The girl finally seemed to agree with him, linking her arm in his, and they walked along the street together. As Marion heard some one walking on the sidewalk, past the big board fence, she had an eager hope that it might be Peter, whistling and walking with his head on one side, but she heard the click, click, clicking of iron cleats—protecting the heels of the shoes, and she knew that Peter didn't wear them. She heard a rustling under the eaves as though some lone city bird or chimney swift had been disturbed and was flapping its wings. From down on the street by the lane that she could not see, came the sound of young fellows' voices, one singing poorly, "I'm in love with a beautiful dame." There was easy laughter from the others. Marion wished they would keep on singing but they passed farther down the street. As she heard the cloppety-clop-clop-clop of a horse on the pavement, she also heard her mother going along the hall to the wash-room.

It may have been only a moment, or a much longer time, when she again heard her mother going back along the hall. Then Marion's throat felt parched, and she wanted a drink, so she moved al-most mechanically from her own room to the hall and to the washroom. As she was lifting the glass to her lips she noticed a cream jar her mother must have left on the basin, a white jar with a black top and a red and silver label, and she picked it up and glanced carelessly at the fine silver printing; it was a special beauty preparation to eliminate puffiness and wrinkles under the eyes.

The angry resentment went out of Marion. "Why, mother's growing old," she thought. "She's old now," and all of her own anger seemed to become ridiculous and was replaced by a feeling of deep humiliation. She thought of her mother as an ageing woman soon to be stooped, and she felt a warm love for her. She was ashamed that she had ever let herself be even faintly jealous.

So she picked up the dainty cream jar, walked along the hall and rapped on her mother's door. "Is that you, Marion; come in, dear," her mother called.

And Marion, smiling at the jar in her hand, real-ized how deep was her mother's pride in her good appearance, and she couldn't bear to humiliate her in this way. "I'll be back in a minute, Mother," she said. She went back to the washroom, put the jar back on the basin, and went to her own room.

In a few moments she heard her mother hurrying in the hall; more slowly she returned again to her own room. Marion followed her.

Mrs. Gibbons was sitting in a rocking-chair in her purple dressing-gown. Her face was without rouge, her skin colorless, even yellow in spots, and large dark circles were under her tired black eyes. Because she had been agitated by her own thoughts, she had taken out of her drawer many of those sensational articles about murders, divorces, seductions, and so on, she saved till she found time to read them. The clippings were spread out on the bed. She had been reading about a man who came home from his work, found his wife drunk on the floor and then kicked her to death with his heavy boots. The predicament of the man startled her and made her forget herself.

She said soberly, with a jerk of her head, "Is there something the matter, Marion, something you want to say to me?" and in her agitation she pulled her dressing-gown tight across her throat.

"No, nothing at all, Mother. We're just not friendly enough, that's all," Marion said, sitting on the edge of the bed. She felt very close to her mother now.

"Well, you're a hard girl to be friendly with."

"Honestly I'm not, Mother. Here, have a cigarette, will you? Let me light it for you."

"It's a little late to try and be friendly," her mother said, puffing the cigarette. "Especially since you're probably thinking of getting married."

"Married. To whom?"

"To Peter, of course."

"Why, I haven't seen him for days. I wouldn't let the boy marry me, even if he wanted to, and apparently he doesn't want to. You and I ought to live together, Mother?" she said, cool and assured.

"You haven't seen him?"

"Not a sight of him."

Almost to herself Mrs. Gibbons muttered, "I wonder what's become of him."

"What did you say, Mother?"

"What are you going to do, Marion?"

"You know what we ought to do, Mother. Two people of our special temperaments ought to get out of the city. It only muddles us. We ought to live in the country. The city gets us mixed up."

"Heavens, Marion, I couldn't stand the country."

Getting up, Marion said, "I'm going to ask Ag to bring us some wine and some biscuits," and she went to the door and called to the maid.

"You don't know what I've been up against, Marion," Mrs. Gibbons said more agreeably. "Your father—a most peculiar man. You're right. Don't marry any one. Are you fond of your father?"

"Well," she said laughing, "I don't think he paid much attention to me."

"He didn't. He depressed me for twenty-five years. Now he's gone away and I don't ever want to see him again."

"Will I pour you a glass of wine, Mother?"

"Please do. A little wine will make me feel better and be good for the spirit as well as the stomach. Thank the Lord for a glass of wine."

"Here you are then, Mother."

"Good health to you, Marion."

As they drank the heavy port wine, for no reason at all, Marion began to talk about Badame, the fruit store Italian, and his little wife with the large bright eyes and the very white skin. Marion said she liked Badame's lazy laugh and the way he wiped his red lips with his hand. "I like thinking about the two of them. They seem to get on so well together," she said.

Mrs. Gibbons jerked her head; her own thoughts seemed to puzzle her, and then she opened her mouth to speak. Shrugging her shoulders, she said, "They keep amused, they keep amused." Hesitating, as if she had been assembling her thoughts while Marion talked about the Italians, she then began to tell fluently about an evening she had spent years ago with her lover, the young army officer, who had been killed in France. "I started thinking about it for some reason when you began talking about Badame and his wife," she said apologetically. It was the first time she had ever conceded that she might have had a lover. Marion, holding her breath, was afraid her mother might shrug her shoulders and stop talking. The young officer and she had been together the evening before he entrained for the seaport, she said; it was the last time she ever saw him. They drove off together in her car to the Don Mills road that leads up through small farmland. It was a warm night in the early summer when the apple trees are beginning to blossom. Before they got out of the car they stopped on the roadside by the trunk of a huge tree. It was a very clear moonlit night. On one side of the road was a field used for pasture and it was just possible to make out the dark forms of cows standing solitary and motionless in the field. Sometimes a cow moved and a bell tinkled, sounding surprisingly loud. At first they couldn't make out where the sound of the bell was coming from, and when they knew they began to laugh. On the other side of the road was an apple orchard, the trees in blossom in fine light clusters in the moonlight. As they sat close together in the car, he began to explain that he was going away to France and might never come back, and since she had never loved any one as much as she loved him, she dug her fingers into his shoulder, put her head down beside him and started to cry. "I felt so sure I was going to lose him," she said. . . . Then it seemed to occur to both of them at the same time to get out of the car and climb through the broken fence to the field. Together they walked through the rows of trees. The air was rich with the smell of blossoms; their shoes sank into the soft mud. In the orchard there seemed to be such an absolute stillness. As he held her arm, she was nervous and trembling; a woman of thirty-five walking at night under the trees in the field with her lover, and not knowing what to expect, seems to be more afraid, more nervous than a young girl. So she was trembling as she walked in the fragrant orchard. They leaned against a tree and he kissed her and said quietly, "This is beautiful here, anyway." They both seemed to feel, by the way he said it, that it was their last time together. "It's so beautiful," she said. And they were silent, not wanting their words to disturb the rapture of what seemed so suddenly to be a holy time. They were both thinking of his dying and of her growing old, and without speaking or moving, they seemed much closer together than they had ever been before. They remained very still, breathing deeply. Up above, through the thick blossoms, they could see small pieces of the moon. They tried to hear the cows moving in the next field and were very glad they had come into the orchard. Subdued, and almost afraid, they walked back slowly to the car. The fair-haired young officer was grave and gentle. "It was so very fine there in the orchard," he said. He spoke as if he knew that once having felt something so beautiful, it was not likely he would ever feel it again. That was the last evening they ever had together. After he had been a month in France he had been killed. "I just mention it," Mrs. Gibbons said apologetically, "because you mention Badame and his wife being so much in love with each other, and besides, I've often tried to figure out why we were so silent and afraid that night. Why nothing happened in the orchard and everything seemed to happen. That's all."

There was a moment of silent close communion between Marion and her mother. In a whisper, Marion said, "You mention the war, and I hardly seem to remember that time. It's all so far away to me. Of course I remember mainly the excitement of armistice time. I went along the streets with other little girls and we cheered and wanted to light bonfires. But I was just a child."

"When I think about it at all, Marion, it still seems dreadfully close to me."

"If it only disturbs you to think about it——"

"I didn't say that. I'll go on thinking about it till the last dog is hung, as we used to say. Yes, you were just a child. I was a young woman then. It bewilders me when I realize the war years went so fast. They swept by and seemed to take everything. I don't mean that. I mean I wish they had actually taken more of me because they've left so much loneliness, a strange kind of inner loneliness. Maybe it's just nostalgia: it must seem sentimental to long for some one you never really knew. In those days I thought I had time to consider everything carefully.

I was the kind of woman who gets confused and says, 'Give me time.' Then years later it seems so unfair that the days, a month, a year was so short. What was it that cheated me? Why should I have to be so swift, Marion?"

"I don't know. I've often cheated myself. When a thing's so close and you want it and you can reach out and touch it, you ought to be swift before you have a chance to cheat yourself."

"That's it, Marion. I was close enough. But I was a timid coward."

"You never were, Mother. I was always a little scared of you because you had so much courage. You might have been reluctant. What could you have done? There was father and there I was, too."

"I know. I know, too, I was close to happiness that would have lasted. But you were just a child and you were very precious to me."

Mrs. Gibbons walked away. Marion followed her to the window, reflecting sadly that it was hard for her even to recall the time that still seemed to hold the core of her mother's life. As they stood shoulder to shoulder, without saying a word, they were looking down at the garden. It was a fine, clear night. Very plainly, Marion saw the garden bench where she had sat with Peter, the lilac tree, and all around the base of the fence, the rosebushes her mother would let no one else touch and had planted and cared for herself. Only the leaves remained on the rosebushes. Red, white and yellow roses had bloomed and fallen a month ago, but yesterday, a white one, blooming later than the others, had blown and the white, withered petals in the clear night were splashed on the dark ground.

Almost afraid to use the words, Marion began to say, "Peter and I . . . I mean it was something the same with us."

"Peter," Mrs. Gibbons said vaguely. "Yes, the trouble was he reminded me of the officer. I made a fool of myself."

"What do you mean, Mother?"

"I got the notion he was fond of me. I seemed to have a whole lot of things mixed up in my head. Then I saw I was a silly old woman."

"Wasn't Peter nice to you?"

"Of course he was. He only smiled. There was no excuse for me. I acted like a silly, sentimental old woman."

"Mother, I love you, I must go now. I must hurry."

"Good-night."

"Good-night, Mother," she said softly. She half smiled with embarrassment: her lips moved, then she threw her arms around her mother and kissed her. "Good-night, good-night," she said.

When she got to her room Marion could no longer subdue her excitement. It seemed that she, herself, in refusing to go away with Peter, was doing what her mother had done when she was a young woman. "Peter, Peter, I've been so foolish. Peter, I love you

so much. I want to be with you forever," she muttered. "I must see you."

It was late but she telephoned to his apartment.
They told her he had moved. Next day she took a
long time to dress and called to see him at his office,
but he was out. She went around to his apartment
house and spoke to the young Jewish writer, who did
not know where Peter had gone. A day later she got
the Windermere Hotel address from the law office,
but it was a Saturday afternoon and he had gone
out for the day.

9

ON Saturday afternoon Peter and Patricia were
taking the radial car out west beyond the city limits
to a place where there were bluffs and hills overlook-
ing the lake. He looked very untidy. For days, in
an effort to get money to keep Patricia, his work had
had no dignity: he had joined those lawyers, the
young and dispirited ones and shabby old ones with
their feet almost bursting out of their worn shoes,
who prowl in the corridors of the county court,
watching for white-faced, worried-looking people
with a summons in their hands. "Have you got
twenty-five dollars?" Peter would say to the worried
ones; then, pocketing the money, he would beg and
plead with the judge about a case he had never heard
of a few minutes before. In the warm summer
months many people took the radial and went out
to the high hills and lay on the grass, waiting for
a breeze. Farm land was farther back from the
bluffs, fields of corn and peas behind low fences.
Peter and Patricia were lying in deep grass by the
edge of the bluffs in the late afternoon. The sun
was far to the west and the water was intensely
blue, just below the bluffs, and farther out, metallic
and shiny. Patricia, smiling sometimes, was silent
and utterly content as she nibbled at a box of
chocolates and read the colored comics of the Sun-

day papers. She was leaning on the news section spread out on the ground, her elbow resting on full-page advice to use "Marlow's Malted Milk, the finest health drink in the whole wide world." Peter was following with his eyes the light slope of the hill to the cornfield and the field of peas behind. Sunlight was shining on stalks and gold tipping the ripe ears of corn. The field of peas was very green.

"Pass me the picture section, Peter?" she said.

"Here you are, Pat," he said. "Never mind it a minute, though. Look up there at the cornfield."

"The cornstalks look fine in the bright sunlight, don't they?" she said.

"It's lovely," he said. "Now look beyond it to the field of green peas."

They lay there looking up at the farm land. The fields were quiet and peaceful and everything was growing. Peter thought with sudden pleasure that the crops were ripening, the soil was exceedingly fertile, seeds had come up out of the ground and in the late summer there was a fulfilment. He looked at Patricia, who was lying lazily on the grass, and he felt a oneness with the hills and bluffs, the lake water and the ripening fields beyond the low fence.

"It reminds me of harvesting time," he said, smiling.

"Harvesting of what?"

"Harvesting of whatever is growing. If you like me, or if there is any kind of feeling growing between us, now is the time for the harvesting. Or maybe I just mean that any man and woman lying here by the ripening fields ought to be in love with each other."

She looked at him and was afraid, for she had none of the feeling inside her that was in him, and the mystery of his sudden interest frightened her a little."Not right here," she said, but she relaxed so that he couldn't help notice her imperturbable grace and massiveness.

"You're right," he said. "I tell you, Pat, let's go up there by the cornfield. Come on, no one will see us."

"Do you think we'd better?" she said. "I was so comfortable lying here, the grass is thick and soft."

"Come on, come on," he said.

So they walked through the grass to the fence by the cornfield and followed it as far back as the field of green peas. The farmhouse was way back from the fields, almost out of sight. Cornstalks would be between them and people who might come down the road. He helped her over the low fence.

In the shadow from the cornstalks in the field of green peas, she said, "This is foolish, Peter; it was far nicer down there by the lake."

"People passing stare at us down there," he said.

"But if my dress is soiled, how will I get home?"

"Such things to worry about. You'll be wearing your coat," he said.

They sat down. Small plants were crushed under her, the green, ripe pods making crunching noises

when she moved. Her neck was curved back and her
head was turned a little to one side. Faint rays of
sunlight coming through the cornstalks fell on the
curve of her neck and glinted on her blonde hair.
Sun shone on the golden corn tassels and the green
plants. Her throat was sloping up to her breast, for
her head was on the ground and her eyes were looking up at the blue sky. Breathing deeply, he filled
his lungs with the clean air and smiled, feeling much
closer to her than he had felt that afternoon in the
hotel room. It seemed good to stretch out, then relax, and know that Patricia, a mature woman, was
contented as she crouched beside him in the field in
so much warm sunlight. Whatever feeling was between them ought to grow and ripen just as the
plants in the field were ripening. He reached out and
touched her hair and then let his hand rest at the
nape of her neck. His eyes were soft and gentle as
he turned to glance at her; then he jerked his head
back: he stared with steady resentment. Her arm
was thrown back behind her head, and her eyes were
rolled so she could see a ripe pod of peas she held
in her hand; with her thumb she was slowly splitting
the pod, and she was absorbed in watching the
shelled ripe peas as they rolled down over her palm
and her wrist to the ground. It was all she was thinking of, and she might have forgotten that he was
there at all. He only shook his head, but he thought,
"What in the world am I doing here with this
woman? There's no real feeling between us," and

with a kind of melancholy bluntness, he said to himself, "I'm a poor fool. Did I think she could make me stop thinking of Marion? Look at her there. She's wondering what's wrong with me. She can't figure it out. Oh, Marion, Marion. I've been trying to hurt you. I've been trying to hurt myself. I feel miles away from here." But he tried hard not to be contemptuous as he said to Patricia, "We're trying to take blood from a stone, Pat. There's simply no feeling between us. Forgive me for saying that. I guess it's my fault." The palm of her hand showed a faint stain from the peas she had crushed. Without moving, she looked up at him, but her face was flushed and she was afraid to speak.

He left her and climbed the fence to walk over to the radial tracks. She followed a few paces behind, her head down, for she was afraid to catch up to him.

When they got on the radial car the corners of his mouth were drooping. A great many kids, carrying picnic baskets, were on the same car and they made a great deal of noise, but Peter, who seemed arrogant and even leaner, looked out the window and felt entirely alone. Patricia was ashamed and still afraid to speak.

Before they got back to the hotel she started to cry a little, but she watched him slyly. "I'm so sorry," she kept on saying. "I love you, Peter. What makes you think I don't? I was thinking about you all the time in the cornfield. I know I don't seem to feel things sometimes." She was pleading with him as though she realized she was going to lose him.

In their room with the green carpet, she sat down and breathed heavily, watching him with furtive glances as he began to pack his bags. "What are you going to do?" she said, following him around the room. "What are you going to do?"

"I'm getting out of here," he said.

"Please, Peter, you can't leave me. What will I do? It was so grand living with you. Please, please, please don't leave me. I'll go to the dogs entirely, you know I will." She kept on trying to put her hands on his shoulders. Then she cried out in a high voice, "You'll be sorry, oh, you'll suffer, just wait," and without waiting even to powder her nose, she ran out. He heard her high heels clicking on the stairs.

In twenty minutes he was packed and ready to leave, and then the phone rang, and Patricia, phoning from the corner drug-store, sounded like a woman who knew she was losing something precious and was trying desperately to hold on. "Oh, Peter," she said, her voice breaking a little. "You're making me do it. I won't go on living. You'll see whether I care for you. I don't want to live. I'm going to kill myself."

"What are you going to do?" he said.

"I'm going to kill myself."

"How?"

"I don't know," she said miserably.

"Then you're wasting your time," he said. "You'd better come home."

"Do you mean it, Peter, do you really mean it?"

"Yes."

"Will you wait there till I come?"

"Yes."

As he put down the phone, he muttered, "The poor girl, she actually talks about loving me more than she does her own life. I won't let her think that." He looked around the room. The bathroom door was open. He went into the bathroom and began to work very rapidly at the medicine chest, but when Patricia came in, he was sitting down, smoking. "Heavens, you look a fright, Pat," he said. "You've got bits of hair hanging down and your nose is actually red."

"Hello, Peter, I came right back. See. Here I am. Oh dear, I can hardly get my breath, I hurried so. Well, it's a corker, it certainly is a corker. That's what I kept saying to myself; it certainly is a corker what's apt to happen. I'll go powder my nose." She hurried into the bathroom. He could see her through the open door.

She was looking at the empty medicine chest, and at the wash-basin that he had heaped with boxes of powder, bottles and toothpastes. She couldn't help looking at the medicine chest again, for two small bottles were left standing close together on one shelf, a bottle of iodine and one of lysol. She was ready to cry as she looked out at Peter, who was smiling.

"Don't you see," he said gently, "a few minutes ago you were going to destroy yourself. Would you though? Would you go ahead and use one of those bottles? It stuns you even to be so close to poison. Well, you can see I didn't mean nearly that much to you, that's all. I didn't want to startle you."

"You wretch, you dog," she screamed after him. "What does any girl mean to you? Get out, you little brat." She flung both bottles wildly and the iodine bottle broke against the wall, leaving a brown blotch on the paper. He was at the door with his bag in his hand when he turned and said, "Good luck, Pat, the best luck in the world to you." She rushed after him. She was a big strong woman quivering with rage, and when she caught up to him, she put both hands up to her head; and then when she saw him standing at the head of the stairs with his back to her, she grew frantic and rushed at him and pushed him with all her weight before he could turn. When she saw him falling down the stairs on his back, she ran into the room and slammed the door.

The desk man with the fat neck, who heard the noise on the stairs, ran over and saw Peter lying with his legs sprawled out awkwardly and his head on the first step. Peter's whole body seemed to be paralyzed. "God help me," he said, trying to move. "God in heaven." The desk man, bending down and puffing, called "Madge, Madge," and the henna-haired little girl from the switchboard appeared, and between the two of them they tried to lift Peter up without hurting him. "Easy now, easy now, let's take it easy," the fat-necked man said. Then the numbness began to go out of the spine. The pain cut off his breath sharply. His legs felt so weak, they hardly seemed to belong to him, but he stood up and started to walk, with the desk man holding his arms. It was like dragging his legs. Breath came whistling through his teeth. "Get me a taxi," he said. "I slipped. No, I've got to go out. Don't take me upstairs. I want a taxi. I want to sit down."

In the cab he tried to lie back and be still. He gave the address of the house by the garage, and then he closed his eyes and wished he would faint, and some one would carry him to a bed. The cab seemed to be floating around in a circle that made him dizzy and weak. But at the apartment house, he got out, white-faced and trembling, paid the man and walked up to the door. The cabman followed with the bags.

To the landlady, he made a deprecating motion of his hand to explain that he wasn't really sick, and he asked shyly if he could have his old room back again. But in the room he crawled over to the bed and lay very still.

Isadore, who was in the next apartment, heard that Peter had returned and he came rushing into the room with both his arms held out and all his teeth showing in a wide-mouthed grin. Throwing his arms around Peter, he said tenderly, "Where have you been, where have you been? You astonish me. You shouldn't do things like that. Look at me, don't I look sad?"

"All of Israel is in mourning."

"Don't start that. Honestly, I haven't done any work since you've been away." Then he added in astonishment, "What's the matter with you? You're hurt. You look sick. You don't move."

"I slipped on a stairs and hurt my back."

"Oh, dear, oh, dear. Here. I'll put your legs on the bed. I'll take off your shoes. I'll talk to you, too. Listen. A swell-looking girl was around here looking for you. Her name was Marion Gibbons. She's lovely. I liked her mouth. I've got a hunch she liked me. She's lovely. Is she your girl?"

"What did she say?"

"She was anxious to see you. I watched her from the window when she went out. She stood on the street looking up and down and I waved to her but she didn't see me."

"Izzy."

"What?"

"Go and phone my brother, will you? Here's the number. He ought to be eating about this time. Tell him to come and see me."

Hubert was frightened when he came to the room, but he would not believe his brother was hurt. Speaking softly and saying how glad he was the affair with the big woman was over, he sat down at the foot of the bed. When Peter said he could walk if he wanted to, but preferred to rest a while, Hubert, who had the utmost confidence in his brother, nodded his head and said it was splendid to be back there in the room listening to the automobiles outside at the station. "I'd like to break that big tart's arm. I knew she'd try and destroy you," he said, and they both laughed, believing that while they were together, nothing could ever destroy them.

"Listen to this," Peter said. "Marion was here. I wonder what she wanted."

"She's a splendid girl," Hubert said quietly. "I could love her all my life. I'll phone her and tell her you're here."

"Wait till to-morrow and we'll see how I feel, and if I'm not better then, we'll get a doctor," Peter said.

10

BUT when Marion saw Peter, fully dressed, lying on the bed and supporting his head with his hand while he smiled so blandly, she forgot everything she intended to say. "Oh, Peter, Hubert says you fell and hurt your back; oh, is it bad?" she said, rushing across the room and kneeling down beside him. She was so full of regret and anxiety that he started to chuckle. He put his hand on her head and kept running it over her thick, glossy hair. For a moment she remained kneeling, feeling her body being suffused with happiness. She closed her eyes, opened them slowly and seemed amazed to find herself there by the bed while his hand caressed her neck. She kissed him, whispering, "I love you, I love you, I'll always love you." She smiled eagerly at Hubert, who was so amused and cheerful.

"Sit on the bed, Marion," Peter said.

"Can't you walk? Have they hurt you very much? They should have hurt me, not you. My Peter, why did you have to get hurt?"

"It's not that bad. I can walk, perfectly, if I insist, but now. . . ."

"It's my fault, so entirely my fault that you're here," she said passionately. "Why didn't we go away? Why didn't you make me go away?"

Smiling a bit, he said, "Why? Because they all

try and stop us, I suppose, the Gods, women on stairs, and whole sets of circumstances."

"Peter."

"What is it, dear?"

"You didn't mention mother. I suppose it was really her fault." Then she added timorously, "But please don't think harshly of her, will you?"

"Why should I?" he said awkwardly, not knowing what to say. "I've always liked your mother."

"I'd like you to see, or just realize, that she's so very eager and sincere."

"I've thought about her," he said at once. "In many ways she is really a deeply religious woman. Anyway, if I'm crocked up, I got what was coming to me for messing around."

Shaking her head, she said, shyly, "I'm glad we understand mother a little better. I mean she's always tried to make her life so vivid and it got pretty miserable. Maybe things beyond her control have spoilt it." Frowning and groping, she said, "Isn't it wonderful how a woman, or anybody for that matter, can keep trying everything and still hunger for something to recall, a few moments with a lover a long time ago?" Then she added, as a kind of apology, "I was thinking of mother and a young officer she loved years ago."

She glanced at Peter, who was looking so childishly pleased with her, and then she looked at his brother, who was beaming with approval. The brothers, expressing such a complete admiration of her, gave her a feeling of humility. Shaking her fair head she said, "How do you like the way I'm doing my hair now?"

"Beautiful. You're so handsome. You never looked so well," they said, almost together.

"It's a little neater when it's straight like this." Quite suddenly she said, "Peter, do you think you're able to go up north to Algoma?"

"Of course I am," he said at once. "Did neither one of you ever have a twisted back? I'll soak it in liniment and rub it and the pain will be gone in two shakes of a dead lamb's tail."

"If we could go . . . maybe we'd better not," she said, growing doubtful.

"We'll go," he said eagerly. "It would be much better resting up there by the lake." He was thinking he ought to move, or he never would, if his spine stiffened.

Hesitating, she said, "Hubert might come and look after us."

"No money," Hubert said, bowing and smiling.

"I'll get you a ticket," she said firmly. "Peter, darling, we'll go at once. We'll wait for nothing. I seem to feel there is so little time."

"The time does seem to go so fast," he said.

"We'll not be afraid. After I heard from Hubert that you were here, I sat down at the piano and tried to play, but I kept saying, 'We'll not be afraid of not having time. We'll go, we'll go.' We could go to-night if you're able to, Peter, sweetheart. We're

hours ahead of train time at midnight. I'd love so
much to get out of here to-night."

Peter, lifting himself with his elbows, stood
up, smiling broadly and held his arms wide for
inspection. "I'll walk up to the corner with you
on your way home to pack, Marion, and I'll show
you the shape I'm in," he said. And he said to
Hubert, "Go on, kid, start packing whatever you
think we'll need, and when I come back we'll go
over to your place."

"I'll do it in jig time," Hubert said, and he
whistled cheerfully as if he felt everything would be
secure now he was going along with them.

Marion and Peter went down the stairs together.
Outside they linked arms and began to walk along
the street. Peter knew she was watching him, so in
an effort to be amusing, he put his heel down, then
slapped his bootsole on the pavement, making a
sharp noise, and Marion began to laugh happily as
though it were the funniest noise in the world. He
kept on doing it till he stopped suddenly. His face
twitched. He said he had stung the sole of his foot
on the pavement. When they were by the street
light she said, "How do you like my new shoes?"
and standing still, she put both her feet together on
the pavement and he looked down at them seriously.
"They're small, neat and beautiful," he said, and
they both regarded the little black patent-leather
shoes with the silver buckles as if they required the
deepest and most attentive consideration, till she

took hold of his hand again and they walked on. He said, "Look at the way that man with the cane walks; doesn't he look funny?" and they both began to giggle as if no one had ever been quite so ridiculous as an innocent, tall man wearing glasses, taking long steps and putting his cane down firmly, on his way home to his wife. They were just feeling good and everybody else seemed very funny. They stood close together in a deep doorway to a darkened building not far away from the brightly lighted corner. They were leaning together and he was bending back every one of her fingers in turn, letting them snap forward, and she was watching him as if much depended upon the springiness of her fingers. The cop on the beat, who was passing, looked in the doorway, stared suspiciously and said, "All right, all right, all right." Marion said impudently, "Go on, hurry home," and the cop, who was startled, began to walk away without once looking back. She had spoken so much like a little street girl that they both began to laugh.

Peter suggested with diffidence that they sit down somewhere and have a cold drink. His legs seemed to be weakening, though he was still smiling. By the corner was an orange-and-black restaurant where they sell mainly soft drinks but provide chairs and tables for people who want coffee and a sandwich. They were sitting in the wicker chairs before she noticed his serious and pale face and his trembling hand. Her eyes grew moist, and she said gently, as she took hold of his hand in her two small hands, "Are you really sure you oughtn't to see a doctor? If you should get hurt, if anything should happen to you now, I'd want to die."

"No," he said, "I ought to rest awhile and not do much walking at a time, that's all. It'll be just right up north."

"Are you very sure, Peter?"

"Didn't I walk with you all right? Weren't you watching?"

She refused to let herself feel uneasy. "You'll be all right, I know," she said. "I can feel it. Please be well. Promise me you will. I'll look after you. I won't let anybody else touch you or help you. If you're hurt and I have to help you, we become so much closer together. It's such a beautiful notion, isn't it? Walking up the street I kept mumbling over to myself words like together and forever and mixing them up and unravelling them. We'll be three whole weeks together. We'll make up for everything we've ever missed. We'll put all our eggs in one basket."

"All our eggs in one basket," he repeated, looking at her eagerly. Then, white-faced and serious, he said, as though frightened, "Promise me you'll never leave me. Swear it."

"There'll be no life for me outside of you. What will I swear by?"

"By something precious and sacred to you. God or Christ."

"You are so precious."

"Swear by life, and death, and beauty, and courage, and hope."

"I swear it. I'll never leave you."

Outside, they called a taxi, and when he got in, he said, "We'll be at the station at eleven-thirty. Don't be late."

"Don't be late," she called out after him as the taxi moved away. She stood on the curb, frowning and looking after the taxi doubtfully. She thought, "Ought we to go? Ought we really to go?" and she was afraid.

11

YET she hummed to herself as she hurried home. In the house she heard her mother moving upstairs and suddenly she listened and felt a reverent tenderness for her. "She's loved so much and so willingly," she thought. All out of breath she rushed up to the bedroom where her mother was sitting by the dressing-table. Mrs. Gibbons had always been a self-possessed, finely preserved woman, bursting with vitality; now her face was unrouged and wrinkled. Her dressing-gown was drawn across her breast. She stared at Marion with uneasy, dark eyes.

"Mother, you look so unhappy. What ails you?"

"I'm going all to pieces, I think," she said, shaking her head.

"Let me do something for you, Mother. Do I seem all out of breath? I rushed up to tell you I'm going away for a week or two to-night."

"Going away. Who with? Where?"

"By myself. Up to Michipicoten on the steamer. It's a little place miles and miles up the lakes."

Mrs. Gibbons' thoughts seemed to puzzle her, for she knew Marion was not telling the truth. "No," she said. "I shouldn't permit that. I haven't been as good a mother as I ought to have been, but I'll try and look after you now." She had a notion that

she wanted to shield Marion, and this emotion con-
soled her. "Ask anything of me, Marion," she said,
shaking her head, "but don't go away and leave me.
We were just starting to love each other." She
frowned as though groping for a sacrifice that would
be an atonement for her whole life. As her lips
moved, she tried not to cry. "Don't go away now
and leave me."

"Mother, I must. I'll be very happy. Don't you
want me to be happy?" But for a moment, she hesitated, feeling a loyal sympathy for her mother
strong above everything. Then, putting her arms
around her, she kissed her quickly, and said,
"Good-bye."

"You're father has left me, and I won't stand for
your going; do you hear, Marion?" She called out
after Marion, "Then please phone your father's
sister for me—Elizabeth Gibbons, the red-headed
one. She's a cheap and spiteful woman, but I won't
be left alone to-night."

"I'll tell Ag to phone, Mother."

"Well, you phone the Cathedral for me, will you,
Marion? I'll have to see a priest."

"No, I won't be so ridiculous. Hold on to yourself, Mother."

"I'll have somebody else do it then," Mrs. Gibbons called after Marion.

For an hour and a half Marion remained in her
own room packing. She heard her father's sister,
Elizabeth Gibbons, come into the house, and she

heard the drone of voices from her mother's room. And just as she finished her packing she heard Miss Gibbons phoning to some one.

She went out without going to her mother's room again, for she had never been friendly with Elizabeth Gibbons. Outside, while waiting for a taxi to pull into the curb, and waiting for the driver to go up the steps and get her bags, she saw the young priest, Father Vincent Sullivan, from the Cathedral, hurrying along the street, his head down in serious concentration. He didn't notice her sitting in the taxi. She smiled when she saw him going into the house to see her mother.

As she watched him going up to the door, she thought uneasily he ought to be told that her mother wasn't feeling well. The young priest looked so grave, he was apt to make her mother think it was a very serious occasion.

"Father," she called softly from the cab, but he did not hear her and was near the door. "Father," she called softly again, but now the taxi driver was apologizing to the priest for bumping into him with her bags. She smiled, then shrugged her shoulders, and did not call again.

At the station, in the waiting-room, Hubert jumped up at once and ran to her as soon as he saw her. Peter, with a solemn face, watched them coming toward him. Finally he stood up and waved his hand deprecatingly. He felt better, he said. But he let her take hold of his arm as they walked down to the train.

On the train she knew he had a very bad night, for he moaned when the train rolled, and she could hear him from her berth across the aisle.

12

FATHER VINCENT SULLIVAN was only one of three curates at the Cathedral, but he had been there long enough to understand that some men and women of the parish deserved to be cultivated more intimately than others. He had some social talent, too. At the seminary, four years ago, he had been lazy, good-natured, and very fond of telling long, funny stories, and then laughing easily, showing his white teeth. He had full red lips and straight black hair. But as soon as he was ordained he became solemn, yet energetic. He never told stories. He tried to believe that he had some of the sanctity that a young priest ought to have. At his first mass, in the ordination sermon, an old priest had shouted eloquently that a very young priest was greater and holier and more worthy of respect than any one else on earth. Father Vincent Sullivan, hearing this, couldn't believe it entirely, but it gave him courage even if it did make him more solemn and serious.

But he still had his red lips and his black hair and his clear skin and a charming, lazy, drawling voice, which was very pleasant when he was actually trying to interest some one. Since he had so much zeal and could be so charming, he was a good man to send calling upon the men and women of the parish, seeking donations for various parish activ-

ities. The really important people in the congrega-
tion like Mrs. Gibbons, whom he bowed to every
Sunday after eleven o'clock mass, he hardly ever
met socially; they were visited usually by the pastor,
who sometimes even had a Sunday dinner with
them or a game of cards in the evening.

Father Sullivan had a sincere admiration for Mrs.
Gibbons. Her donations were frequent and generous. She went regularly to communion, always
made a novena to the Little Flower, St. Teresa. And
sometimes in the summer evenings, when he was
passing down the aisle from the vestry and it was
almost dark in the Cathedral, he saw this good
woman saying a few prayers before the altar of the
Virgin. Of course he hardly glanced at her as he
passed down the aisle, his face grave and expressionless, but he thought about her when he was at the
door of the church and wished that she would stop
and talk to him, if he stayed there, when she passed
out. She was the kind of a woman, he thought, that
all the priests of the parish ought to know more intimately. So he did happen to be near the door, but
she went by him and down to the street, hardly
more than nodding. She was a large, plump, well-
kept woman, walking erectly and slowly to the
street. Her clothes were elegant. Her skin had been
pink and fine. It was very satisfactory to think that
such a well-groomed, dignified and competent
woman should appreciate the necessity of strict religious practice in her daily life. If he had been

older and had wanted to speak to her he could
readily have found some excuse, but he was young
and fully aware of his own particular dignity. Honestly, he would rather have been the youngest priest
at the Cathedral at this time than be a bishop or a
cardinal. It was not only that he always remembered the words of the old priest who had preached
his ordination sermon, but he realized that he sometimes trembled with delight at his constant opportunity to walk upon the altar, and when hearing
confessions he was scrupulous, intensely interested,
and never bored by even the most tiresome old
woman with idiotic notions of small sins. It exalted
him further, even if it also made him a little sad, to
see that older priests were more mechanical about
their duties, and when he once mentioned it to
Father Jimmerson, the oldest priest at the Cathedral, the old man had smiled and sighed and said it
was the inevitable lot of them all, and that the most
beautiful days of his life had been when he was
young and had known the ecstasy of being hesitant,
timid and full of zeal. Of course, he added, older
priests were just as confident in their faith, and just
as determined to be good, but they could not have
the eagerness of the very young men.

At about nine o'clock, when Father Sullivan was
sitting in the library reading a magazine, the house-
keeper came into the room and said that some one,
phoning from Mrs. Gibbons' house, wanted to speak
to a priest.

"Was any priest in particular asked for?" Father Sullivan said.

"No. The woman—I don't know who she was— simply said she wanted to speak to a priest."

"Then I'll speak to her, of course," Father Sullivan said, putting aside his magazine and walking to the telephone. He was delighted at the opportunity of having a conversation with Mrs. Gibbons. He picked up the receiver and said, "Hello."

A woman's voice, brusque, practical, said, "Who's that?"

"Father Sullivan," he said encouragingly.

"Well, I'm Mrs. Gibbons' sister-in-law, and I'm at her house now. Things have come to a pretty pass around here. If you've got any influence, you ought to use it. Just at present Mrs. Gibbons is broken up thinking she's going to die and she's been howling for a priest. There's really nothing wrong with her, but if you've got any influence you ought to use it on her. She's a terrible woman. Come over and talk to her."

"Are you sure?" he said a bit timidly.

"Sure of what?"

"Sure that you're not mistaken about Mrs. Gibbons."

"Indeed, I'm not. Are you coming?"

"Oh, yes, at once," he said.

He put on his hat and looked at himself mechanically in the hall mirror. Then he glanced at his hands, which were perfectly manicured and clean.

His collar was spotless. The blood showed through his clear skin and his lips were very red.

As he walked along the street he was a little nervous because the woman had sounded so abrupt, and he was wondering uneasily if Mrs. Gibbons really was a terrible woman. There had been some rumors of a certain laxity in her life since her husband had either disappeared or deliberately gone away some time ago, but the pastor had shrugged his shoulders and spoken of scandalmongers. Insinuations against the good name of Mrs. Gibbons, who, they knew, was one of the finest women of the parish, were in a measure an insinuation against the Church. Father Sullivan had decided some time ago that Mrs. Gibbons was really a splendid woman and a credit to any community.

It was a short walk from the Cathedral to Mrs. Gibbons' home. A light was in the hall. A light was in the front room upstairs. Father Sullivan paused a moment at the street light, looking up at the house, and then walked quickly up to the door, feeling clean, aloof, dignified and impressive, and at the same time vaguely eager.

He rang the bell. The door was opened wide by a woman, slim, brightly dressed, florid-faced, and with her hair dyed red, who stepped back and looked at him critically.

"I'm Father Sullivan," he said apologetically but seriously.

"Oh, yes, I see."

"I believe Mrs. Gibbons wanted to see me."

"Well, I don't know whether she knows you or not," the woman added a bit doubtfully. "I'm her sister-in-law. I'm the one that phoned you."

"I'll see her," he said with a kind of grave finality as he stepped into the house. He felt cool, dignified and important.

"I mean that I was going to talk to you first," the red-headed woman said. "She's a tartar, you know—only it just happens that she feels broken up now about something, and it's time for some one to give her a talking to."

"I'll talk to her," he said. Really he didn't know what he was expected to say.

The slim woman walked ahead upstairs and Father Sullivan followed. The door of the front room was open and the slim woman stood looking into the room. The light shone on her red hair. Father Sullivan was close behind and followed her into the room. Mrs. Gibbons was lying on a divan, a purple kimono thrown loosely around her. One of her plump arms was revealed as she held her head up, resting on her elbow. Her plump body was hardly concealed under the kimono. She looked depressed and unhappy as though she had been crying. When she saw Father Sullivan she didn't even open her mouth, just shrugged her shoulders and held the same dejected expression. The red-headed, slim woman stared at her alertly and then glanced at Father Sullivan, who was bending forward trying to attract Mrs. Gibbons' attention while he got ready to speak in his slow, drawling, and pleasing voice. But then he noticed a wine bottle on the table close to the divan. Mrs. Gibbons was now looking at him curiously, and then she smiled. "Can't ask you to have a drink, Father," she said. She was obviously thinking what a nice young fellow he was. Then she started to laugh a little, her whole body shaking.

"I thought you wanted to talk to him, Tessie," the other woman said.

"Oh, I don't think I do."

"But you said you wanted to."

"Oh, Father won't mind; will you, Father?"

"Go on, talk to her, Father," the red-headed woman said impatiently. "Something's bothering her conscience. I've been trying to tell her what a trollop she is. You tell it to her."

If Mrs. Gibbons had started talking to him, Father Sullivan might not have been embarrassed, but as he looked at her, waiting, and saw her stretched out so carelessly and noticed again the wine bottle on the table, he felt he was going to hear something that would disgrace her and the parish forever. She kept on looking at him, her underlip hanging a little, her eyes old and wise. The red-headed woman was standing there, one hand on her hip, her mouth drooping cynically at the corners. They were both waiting for him to say something. In the darkness of the confessional it would have been different, but now Father Sullivan felt his face flushing, for he couldn't help thinking of Mrs. Gibbons as one of the finest women of the parish, and there she was stretched out like a loose old woman. He tried to hold his full, red lower lip with his white teeth. He felt humiliated and ashamed and they were both watching him. His nervous embarrassment began to hurt and bewilder him.

"She took a bit to drink after eating a heavy meal, so she got a slight attack of acute indigestion, I think," the red-headed woman said. "She feels better now, but she's still slightly under the weather. Look at her."

Mrs. Gibbons, with her hands at her breasts, was shaking her dark head wearily. She seemed to be contemplating herself growing old, her hands, her neck, her ankles once so slender and her face once so round and smooth. And as if seeing her sister-in-law, the red-haired Elizabeth Gibbons, for the first time, she said bitterly, "So you were talking to me about never being good to my husband and being loose. A gadabout like you. What's the use of telling you it was his disposition that ruined our life together. At first I used to feel sorry for him and think he couldn't help his jealous nature, then I got to hate him. I couldn't help it; he led me a perfect dog's life from the time I had been married to him a few months. He was scared of something, perhaps. I never could quite figure him out. Something was in him like a devil distorting everything. I remember

when we used to go to a show, he'd hardly look at
the stage, he'd be looking slyly at me and then at
any man who happened to be sitting near us, to see
if I might be flirting. I actually used to feel sorry
for him. But I stopped going to the theatre with
him. I didn't go to a theatre for over two years.
But if it wasn't that, it was something else. I used
to love dancing and sometimes he'd take me to a
ball, but he stopped that, too. He'd find the most
idiotic excuses, like when I was all dressed and excited, ready to go to the ball, he'd find something to
delay us; he'd even invent excuses to stop us going
at the last moment. I don't think he wanted me to
meet any one I might like. I felt hunted. You know
he hardly ever opened his mouth either, while he
went on dogging me. I suppose you know all that,
Elizabeth? Never mind. I'll tell you something,
Elizabeth, I'm going away. I'm going to France and
I'm going to live there. Loyalty, loyalty to some
one, at least, Elizabeth. Who is the young man
standing beside you? Oh, yes, the priest."

"You wanted a priest," the red-headed woman
said, and she whispered to Father Sullivan, "Better
plug your ears, Father."

"If I can be of any assistance——" he muttered,
feeling almost ready to cry.

They didn't speak to him, just kept on looking
at him steadily and he had a sudden nervous feeling that the red-headed woman might go out and
leave him alone with Mrs. Gibbons.

Some words did actually come into his head, but Mrs. Gibbons, sitting up, stared at him and said flatly: "Oh, he's too young. How do you expect me to talk to him?" Then she lay down again and looked away into the corner of the room.

The sister-in-law took hold of Father Sullivan firmly by the arm and led him out to the hall. "She's right about that," she said. "I thought so from the start."

"There are some things that are hard to talk about, I know," he said, flustered and ashamed. "If in her life . . . . I mean, I have the greatest faith in Mrs. Gibbons," he said desperately. "Please let me go back and talk to her."

"No. I sized up the situation and know that once she got talking to you she'd pull the wool over your eyes."

"I was just about to say to her—" Father Sullivan said, following her downstairs, and still trembling a little—"I know she's a good woman."

"No, you're too young for such a job. And she hasn't the morals of a tomcat."

"I ought to be able to do something."

"Oh, no, never mind, thanks. She's got over the notion she's going to die. I could tell that when she shrugged her shoulders."

"But please explain what she wanted to say to me," he said. "I respect Mrs. Gibbons," he added helplessly.

"It's no use—you're too young a man," the woman

said abruptly. "You wouldn't be able to do anything with her anyway."

"I'm sorry," he said. "I'm awfully sorry," he kept
on saying. She had hold of his arm and was actually
opening the front door. "Thanks for coming, anyway," she said. "We've been rowing and I told her
plenty and I wanted some one else she respected to
take a hand in it."

"I'm very sorry," he said. "Was she feeling
badly?"

"Pretty badly. I came around here, when she
phoned me, to give her a piece of my mind, but she
was all broken up. Something got into her."

"Something must have happened, because she's a
fine woman. I know that."

"You do, eh? Her daughter Marion has gone
away with her young man, Peter."

"I didn't know the daughter very well," the priest
said.

"No? Well, it looks to me as if Tess wanted to
know Peter too well. That was the trouble, and
it's bothering her conscience now. When I came
around here she was lying down half dressed looking
at herself in a hand mirror. What's the matter with
her? She's got to grow old some time. Thanks,
though, for coming. Good-night."

"Good-night. I'm sorry I couldn't help her."

As he walked down the street he had a feeling
that the woman might take him by the arm and
lead him down to the corner.

It was a mild, warm night. He was walking very slowly. The Cathedral spire stuck up in the night sky above all the houses in the block. He was still breathing irregularly and feeling that he had been close to something immensely ugly and evil that had nearly overwhelmed him. He shook his head a little, because he still wanted to go on thinking that Mrs. Gibbons was one of the finest women in the parish, for his notion of what was good in the life in the parish seemed to depend upon such a belief. And as he walked slowly he felt, with a kind of desperate clarity, that really he had been always unimportant in the life around the Cathedral. He was still ashamed and had no joy at all now in being a young priest.

13

IN the early morning they arrived at the Soo and had to wait a few hours before they could go on board the steamer, so they went down to the dock, and had a small lunch and waited. Peter was irritable. It was such an effort for him to walk that both Hubert and Marion thought he would faint. "It's my fault for bringing you up here," she kept on saying. "You ought to be in bed and have a doctor." The three of them sat on a bench by the dock, watching the steamer and waiting. Marion had looked after the tickets, for she was the only one who had any money.

On the steamer the brothers had one stateroom. There was a heavy fog in the morning and the water was very choppy. When Marion went into the brothers' stateroom, she saw Hubert sitting on the end of the lower berth, looking at Peter, who had his eyes closed. As soon as Peter heard her, he tried to smile and put out his hand, and she felt uneasy. "What's the matter, dear boy; doesn't it feel any better at all to-day?"

"It seems to want to stiffen," he said, "so when I move it hurts pretty badly."

"It'll get better," she said.

"Oh, certainly. It's probably a kind of sprain," Hubert said. "He'll get better."

In the small, white room the three of them felt very close together and necessary to each other.

"If it's paining," she said, "I know I couldn't stand it. I'm such a little coward."

"Oh, sure you could," Peter said.

"Do you mind me putting my hand on your head?"

"Oh, no, your hand is so fine and cool."

"There's a scratch on the side of your face, too," she said. "I'm the one that ought to be smashed up. I'm the one that's bringing us up here."

"I'm glad we're here," he said simply.

On the deck she walked by herself. Ahead of her were three young girls, making the north shore trip, who were dressed in red pajamas and little striped sweaters. The steamer was going forward steadily into the dull gray mist. Short, choppy waves thudded against the boat side. But suddenly the sun shone through the gray mist and the dark water became very blue. Away to the right was the rolling shore line, still half banked in heavy mist. Marion walked by herself till she encountered the ship's doctor, an Englishman with an aquiline nose and expressionless face. Casually she told him that Peter had fallen and hurt his back and it appeared he would not be able to enjoy the boat trip. "What a shame," he said. "What a shame. Should I take a look at him?"

"Please, if you would."

After a casual examination, the doctor shook his

head doubtfully. How far were they going? To Michipicoten. My, my, my, my, my! It would be so extraordinarily painful for the young man. Did the young man feel great pain at the moment? Mainly when he moved. There was no knowing how seriously he was hurt till they X-rayed him, but there was the bad bluish-red welt on his back, though, of course, he had been able to move his legs, so far. It looked as if one of the vertebræ was hurt, but that the cord hadn't been severed. Of course, if the cord had been severed he would have been paralyzed at once. One was reluctant even to say that he could go on in such a condition, but he actually could till the pain brought him down. Usually, if there was to be paralysis, it occurred at once, but that was because the cord was severed. With one of the vertebræ hurt, and the young man going on, anything was likely to happen. The chief danger would probably be from a hemorrhage that would follow, and from that, a paralytic condition might develop. But it was good that he had been able to move his legs so far. The last thing on earth he would care to do would be to alarm them unduly, for, after all, one could offer no final explanation without an X-ray. That was something. Peter really oughtn't to be moved at all; the only thing to do was rest and hope nothing had happened; it might just be a sprain, it was hard to say. "Let us hope his spine isn't hurt," he said.

"Should he stay here in bed?" Hubert asked.

"Oh quite, quite," the doctor said, speaking positively for the first time.

So Marion went up to the deck with the doctor and found it very hard to get rid of him. She was bored because he had nothing to say; he was just so very polite and respectful. His was a very empty and placid life, so now he kept glancing with grave admiration at Marion's profile, and seemed frightfully confused when she detected him. They were standing by the rail, looking toward the shore. Once he had known a man, he said, who had slipped on a stairs and hurt his back, but the remarkable part of it was that the man had really hurt a small bone in his neck. Fancy that. You never could tell about such things. This man he knew had forgotten about the fall on the stairs, but just the same he had kept on twitching his neck for the rest of his life. Such talk didn't greatly disturb Marion, for she thought the doctor an amiable fool, but the heavy feeling inside her began to hurt and soften her. Her full red lower lip began to tremble. Out of this trip she had expected a great deal of happiness and now she felt so utterly alone as she looked toward the shore and the Algoma Hills. Between great dark wooded hills were sharp ravines still filled with mist, and only the rocky summits of the hills reached up to the sunlight. And even the water lapping on the side of the boat seemed to upset her. "I'll have to move some place where I can't hear that lapping," she thought, for she knew she was afraid. The doctor, his head leaning out over the rail with the water as a background, was smiling till his expressionless face was all wrinkled up. "But I know there isn't anything to worry about," she thought, and as she looked down at her ankles, she noticed the doctor, too, glancing down, and the blood seemed warm within her. Closing her eyes, she thought eagerly of being alone with Peter, and almost shyly let herself think of him loving her while her lips parted and her eyes felt moist. The lake, the shoreline, the foolish doctor no longer had any interest for her; she wanted all of it to slip by.

"They say the hills are just like the Pyrenees in Spain," the doctor was saying politely.

"They are beautiful."

"Are you really so very happy?" he said, surprising even himself, for he never spoke out so directly.

"Oh, yes, thank you. Do I look so contented?" she said, feeling her face crimsoning, and she began to walk away lazily.

"Quite, quite," he said, looking after her, as though he had been startled by the tender expression on her face. As she walked away with a curious aloofness, the wind was blowing back her blonde hair and he felt the single question had been an intrusion. He felt almost excited himself, for some reason.

At noon time she had lunch with Peter and Hubert in the stateroom. With an absurd apologetic grin, Peter said, "This is so very silly. I could walk, you know, but that silly doctor says my back will be better later on if I rest."

When Hubert had left them alone, she said, "Peter, Peter, I want to be so happy with you."

"Are you feeling happy now?"

"Yes, I'm very, very happy."

"And aren't we going to have such a good time together?"

"Oh, we must. I've been thinking of the little things we'll do. Not the important things, just the little trivial things. We'll take sunbaths on the rocks, and we'll listen and see how many bird-calls we know."

"Is it a very silent country?"

"It is. The smallest sounds, the fluttering of a bird's wings sound loud."

"That's splendid. We'll wake up at night when it will be black out, and we'll lie there, and it will seem so black and dark and we'll feel so terribly close together."

"Oh, we will. We'll make a bundle of all our thoughts and our pleasures, and make a grand bonfire."

"This is our trip," he said. "All our eggs in one basket, remember that."

Then she kissed him and bent down over him, and he said, "I like that. I like it." And she put his shoes on for him because he decided that if he was ever going to get off the boat, he might as well get used to moving at least on the deck. "Wait till you see me walk off the boat," he said, smiling cheerfully, though moving very slowly.

He sat on the deck in the late afternoon for over an hour. The three of them sat together in deckchairs, and Marion, holding Peter's hand under the blanket, felt such an extraordinary peace and contentment. She held her breath for fear of disturbing it. Hubert was smoking his pipe. Nothing they could have said would have made them feel any closer together. All afternoon it was calm and clear on the water, the hills and shoreline receding till there was only the blue sky and the blue lake, and far behind on the horizon one great white bank of clouds rolling like white winter hills.

In the evening Marion and Hubert sat on the deck, talking and at the same time feeling they were merely waiting for Peter to come up, when they both knew they had persuasively insisted that he remain below. They tried to talk to each other as if nothing had disturbed them. Forward, on the deck, was the ship's orchestra and dancing, girls laughing boisterously; some, who had been drinking too much, very noisy. Deck lights polished the surface of the dark water. Hubert was amusing Marion, telling her about Elsie Saunders, a widow with a twelve-year-old son, the woman he loved. Smiling and talking without passion, as if he could see her there clearly before him, he said that in one way she was like a great many other small, dark, plump

women. He had seen her for the first time on a
street car with her boy, who was carrying a violin
and wearing an Eton collar with a black bow-tie.
To him she had looked something like a flower that
had been waiting a long time for the sunlight so it
could open out and bloom sweetly. Her husband,
he found out later, had been a foreman in an auto-
mobile plant before he died. The trouble was the
factory had slowly drawn his life into it till he got
to be like a machine, and it began to have the same
effect on her. Before he became a foreman he worked
with men doing piece work in the line in the factory;
the line formed at seven-thirty and all day there
was the mental strain of keeping up with production and the steady grind against the line. At the
end of the line in the floor was a hole with a hoist
in it. When a finished chassis is under a hole they
must drop a body on it, or all the men doing piece
work would be held up. "Imagine holding up production. That's the greatest sin in the world now-
adays," Hubert said with mock seriousness. Anyway, if production were to be held up the production
manager would come around and some men would
lose their jobs. Supposing a man in the line was
trying in vain to insert a defective nut or screw; he
has to work twice as hard to recover his lost ground,
or lose his place in the line when men, working just
as frantically as he, would push him aside and curse
him for holding them back. A guy couldn't have
any pleasant little moments for bumming, or talk-

ing, when no man could leave the line unless the foreman was there to take his place."

"Sounds like a lot of galley slaves," Marion said.

"Well, it's really worse in a way," Hubert said. "It begins to affect their whole life without their noticing it. If they were working with their hands on wood or metal they could see the product of their labor and take pride in it, but the division of labor has spoilt that." He went on to say that Mrs. Saunders' life became just as methodical as the life at the factory. Of course, Hubert admitted, laughing, he must have at some time or other made love to his wife, for she did have the child. "But what I wanted to say," Hubert said, "is that for a long time this woman couldn't understand why I bothered to caress her, for lovemaking had no enchantment in it for her. She had a sympathetic nature and didn't mind my wanting to love her. But whenever I touched her very tenderly, as though she were precious, she seemed bothered and wanted to cry.

"Is she still that way?" Marion said, smiling as though she knew the answer.

"Lord, no. She's used to me and it's just as though a new life has begun for her," he said with modest pride.

"I'll bet she loves you. You're very nice, you know."

Looking at her, he said, "Maybe by to-morrow, if Peter is quiet, his back won't hurt him."

"I only hope there's some kind of a doctor somewhere near the Mission," she said. "There'll be one up at the Falls, maybe. But he'll be all right, don't you think, Hubert?"

"Oh, absolutely," he said, smiling confidently. A light overhead was shining on his round, serious face, and as he fumbled for his pipe, he even laughed a bit, implying that it was ridiculous to think of anything upsetting Peter permanently.

14

IT was late in the afternoon when the steamer crossed the wide mouth of the Michipicoten River and passed the yellow sandbar, and the point of black jutting rock. At the dock there was a small shed, a government warehouse and a dirt road leading back through the wooded hills. On a small sandy beach littered with washed-up and sun-baked wood, five round squat Indian women sat huddled together on a log, their black shawls over their shoulders, watching passengers get off the steamer for an hour's walk on the sand. The boat would remain at the dock till supplies were unloaded and then go farther on up the north shore.

Marion and the two brothers stood on the narrow dock looking for some one who might be going up to the Mission. Though Hubert twice tried to take hold of his arm, Peter stubbornly refused assistance, and stood to one side, staring with great curiosity at the great black slabs of rock jutting out into the lake. The whole country seemed to be solid black rock covered with thin surface earth for roots.

Marion, looking around, was delighted by her own eagerness. She had been looking forward for so long to standing on the dock with Peter, breathing the crisp clean air of this country, that now it didn't matter at all that he was hurt. If he had been abso-

lutely helpless at the moment, there still would have
been a satisfaction for her in being there. The three
of them were on the dock together. A big truck
came down the dirt road from the Falls and the men
got off, prepared to load iron rails and take them up
to the construction camp; they were harnessing the
Falls. The very blue lake water was being spoiled
by the garbage which was being tossed from the
boat.

To the white-headed, white-shirted, and very sun-
burnt man who was standing by the warehouse with
his hands on his hips, Marion said, "Is there some
one who could take us up to the Mission?"

"There's a fellow with a boat at the end of the
dock there. Why not ask him?" the man said. "His
name is Steve. He lives up there. He's the fellow
in the gold and purple sweater."

Tied to the end of the dock was an old motorboat
used for trolling. A fellow in a gold and purple
sweater, the stripes running lengthwise like the
stripes in an English soccer player's sweater, and
the sweater hanging loosely down to his hips, was
sitting on a pile of new lumber with three other
fellows. His face was richly copper-colored and he
wore a black hat like a ball player's. His eyes were
hazel and slow moving. Sitting on the pile of wood,
the men were silent, immobile, looking straight out
over the calm blue water, their hands linked around
their knees, as if they could sit on there forever
without moving or speaking, and yet without even

glancing at the brothers, or Marion, they were aware of them, and aware of her approaching and smiling nervously. They didn't have many chances to look closely at soft city women.

When Marion spoke to Steve, he raised his hat politely, and his voice was extraordinarily soft. "I'd like to go up to the Mission to Bousneau's boarding house. Do you think you could take us?" she said.

"I'll be glad to," he said as he slid down from the pile and walked along the dock to get their bags. When Hubert saw him picking up the bags, he, too, insisted upon carrying one, and as they walked along to the boat, he tried to make a pleasant conversation. The fellow hardly answered at all. It was easier to get into the boat by going down the black rock slope because the jagged edges were like steps. Steve, with his hand under Marion's elbow, helped her step to the boat, and then he watched Hubert, who was helping Peter. But a wave lapped against the boat, swaying it away just as Peter stepped to it stiffly, and so his body lurched off balance and he gasped with the pain in his spine. And finally Peter sat erect in the open boat, holding his lips close together while he tried to prevent his body from trembling. The man in the bright soccer-player's sweater looked at him with a great deal of sympathy in his soft brown eyes as he tinkered with his old engine and the boat slowly curved around the steamer, heading for the rocky point that divided the river mouth from the small beach at the dock.

As soon as they were off the shore and could feel the river current rocking the boat the two brothers seemed to relax, but they sat there, silent. Marion, sitting forward, looked carefully at the two brothers and smiled. Hubert looked sturdy and alert and healthy; Peter, who had taken out his handkerchief to mop his sweating forehead, was holding the pain in him, unyielding, independent, determined not to be hurt; and yet, sitting there in the boat, he seemed to feel by his own silence that his small lean body and his determination were suddenly pitiful on such a wide water with the vast reddening sky and the black rocky faces of the great rugged hills. The country could not give him the strength he had expected; sitting there, it was as though his resistance, the core of him, was dissolving till even his pain was unimportant.

Marion, whose underlip was drooping, was staring, with her impenetrable blue eyes, at Steve, who was sitting by himself almost huddled over his engine, watching it carefully. His trousers hung on him loosely and she imagined his body was lean and wiry. Sometimes he looked for a long time far over the lake, as if he never expected to see anything on the water, nothing but the horizon on the wide sweep of water, and so was content. Faint streaks of gray were at the temples in his jet-black hair. His features were straight and firm. As he sat there, huddled down and silent, his ridiculously bright sweater seemed to give comic emphasis to his melancholy peacefulness. He had been born in this country, had a boy by a wife who was dead, had sent him to school in Michigan, and had once gone to Detroit to live, but had finally returned to go on with his fishing at the Mission.

"I was up here two years ago," Marion said suddenly.

"Yes, mmm," he said.

"But I don't remember you."

It was difficult making a conversation because of the put, pit, put-put of the engine. They were rounding the point and heading up the river. Away to the right, where the river waters met the lake, there was, for two miles, a long sandy beach, the sun shining on it till it glistened like a great polished bone set down between the blue water and the green hills.

Going up the river they passed one big house on the right bank, the old Hudson Bay trading post, and after they had passed the curve in the river, they saw ahead, where the hills opened out for a small tributary river, the Mission on the hill, two rows of wooden houses, a small white church, a general store with a big false front, a dilapidated, rotting dock, and an old worm-eaten fishing boat, keeled over and half buried in the mud and thick water weeds. Weeds were so thick on the surface by the plank dock, the water could hardly be seen.

"Why don't they clean out the weeds?" Peter said, speaking irritably.

"What for?" Steve said mildly.

They had to go up the steep bank to the boarding house, which was just to the left of the general store at the top of the bank.

Marion tried to help Peter out of the boat, feeling, for some reason, a marvelous tenderness for him, as if she would be content simply to watch him sleeping. From up the tributary river came the sound of a waterfall. She balanced herself on the rotting dock planks and reached down her hands to Peter, smiling warmly, and Hubert stood back, grinning. But her foot slipped slightly; her shoe dragged in the water, pulling out a yellow weed, and she felt with strange nervousness that she would be helpless in such a country. She looked up at the steep bank, marked by many footprints, and down at the hulk rotting in the water. The river water never moved. Thick weeds were like a great net holding down the life in the river. It felt so good to her to see, suddenly, far down the river, past the turn, a bit of sunlight on the dark swirling water. Then she felt like a kid for feeling worried because her foot had slipped into the water.

Hubert and Steve were helping Peter climb the bank. But Peter was bending forward; he sank to his knees, his lips trembling, and when they lifted him up again, his legs seemed to swing loosely from his hips. "Don't move me," he said, very angry. "I can't make that hill, I tell you. Oh, Jesus," he gasped, and then, helpless, he looked at Márion.

"It's my fault, Peter," she said. "It's my fault. I shouldn't have made you come up here. I'm so selfish." And she did think herself a silly, selfish woman, as she looked at him with her mouth hanging open, longing to feel some of his pain inside her. "Forgive me, Peter," she said. "I'm so sorry." She was holding her small fists tightly together, and looking all around to see something that might help her; in her there had been a plan, but now the plan seemed to have belonged entirely to some one else, to an assertive, confident woman. She wanted to sit down on the sandy slope of the hill. And she felt if she and Peter could only sit there alone on the bank, somehow, they would feel much better.

"I can't go any farther," he said.

"I honestly never thought it hurt so much, Peter," she said contritely. She bent down and brushed her cheek against his face, and seemed to have decided to go no farther. But Steve said, "I guess he's pretty bad."

"Can't we carry him?" Hubert said.

"We'll carry him up to the boarding house," Steve said, and he wanted to ask why on earth they had come so far.

Hubert had spoken confidently, but without any of his boyish earnestness, for his face was white and he was alert. Steve helped him carry Peter; they each put an arm under his armpits, and carried him easily without swaying the body at all. As she followed up the bank Marion couldn't bear to look at

his shoes dragging loose on the sand. The light,
black-polished shoes were dragged up the bank over
the sand.

Marion went on ahead to speak to some one at
the boarding house. In the kitchen, at the back of
the house, Bousneau, a great fat man, nearly seven
feet tall, was having an argument with his wife, but
he came to the screen door, waving his pipe, and
after peering at Marion, he remembered her from
two years ago. "Why it seems weeks since I got your
letter," he said. "Oh, ma, ma, come here a minute,
ma." Then he saw that Marion was trembling, almost mute, as she looked at him. Shaking her head,
she couldn't seem to find any words; then she regained her self-assurance, and while he looked at her
a bit stupidly with his mouth open, she said, twisting one corner of her lip, "Here we are, Mr. Bousneau. There are three of us. One of my friends hurt
his back and it's been getting worse." She spoke
with a sort of lazy indifference.

Bousneau stood beside her on the porch watching
the three men coming up the road. Peter was now
walking by himself with a slow, wavering step.
Steve, carrying the three bags effortlessly, lagged a
bit behind.

"You'll be wanting a dinner," Bousneau said.
"I've got two rooms. Your friends can have one
and you the other."

"And is there a doctor around?"

"There might be one up at the Falls, but not

likely. You could get one down from Hawk Junction. Steve could go down to the dock and tell the boys who are loading to arrange it when they go back."

Bousneau was very jolly, very boisterous, very helpful. His small nose and mouth were almost lost in his enormous face. He showed them their rooms; he introduced his wife, slapping her on the back and explaining that she was a good woman; indeed she was, he having lived entirely on her work in the boarding house for six years. It was the only boarding house for miles and miles, so he was able to eat heartily, sleep in the afternoons and sometimes go fishing at twilight. . . . From the porch Marion called to Steve, who was walking down the dirt road to his shack. The late sun, just dropping behind the hills, was shining on the back of his neck, and he looked very slender; the fine black hair was long on the nape of his neck. Alert, he turned when she called and came back to the house looking straight at her with his soft, dark eyes.

"Would you ask some one over at the dock to try and get me a doctor?" she said.

"Yes, ma'am," he said. "The truck they're loading over at the dock will be going back in an hour. I'll go right over."

"Thank you, Steve. You're a good fellow. Where do you live?"

"In the shack straight down at the end of the road."

"You'll always help us. Won't you?"

"Oh, sure," he said, smiling and speaking softly.

Upstairs, in the room she had for herself, Marion began to take her clothes out of her bag and hang them on the wire hooks on the door, and sometimes she listened intently for small sounds from the brothers' room. Two or three times she heard Peter groaning, and Hubert's voice rising and falling. And when her heart began to beat so loudly she could not get her breath, she went into the next room and saw Peter lying on the bed with his eyes closed. Hubert, looking big, awkward and eager, put his hand on his brother's head and said, "He's a bit feverish. That's excitement and worry more than anything else. He'll be all right."

"I sent for the doctor. I just wanted to see how he was now."

Without opening his eyes, Peter put out his hand to her and she raised it and touched it to her lips. As she sat down at the foot of the bed and kept on looking at Hubert's round, calm, earnest face, she wanted very much to talk to him, but knew he thought his brother ought to sleep. Shadows were lengthening in the room. She couldn't stand the silence, so she withdrew her hand, smiled at Hubert, and went back to her own room and sat down by the window looking out over the small weedy bay. It was getting darker. She could see far down the river, almost as far as the old trading post.' Some one, a thin boy with a ragged peak cap, and an old coat four sizes too large for him, was coming along the dirt road past the row of houses. She heard faintly the thud of iron bars being piled on the truck over at the dock. Sounds carried for miles over the hills. As she looked down the river valley the last sun rays, shining on the smooth running water, shone brightly on Steve's golden-striped sweater as he sat huddled over his engine, while the old boat went skimming around the point. "I forgot to pay him for bringing us up here," she thought, when she could no longer hear the pit, put, pit-put-put of the engine.

She was aroused when Hubert rapped on the door. Grinning boyishly, he seemed to have recovered all his assurance. While he was lighting his pipe she couldn't help laughing. "You're a dear," she said, putting her arms around him and hugging him.

"Peter's asleep," he said. "We'll go down and eat with the portly gent."

For some reason she felt ashamed of herself and began to explain that she had been feeling upset from thinking of Peter being helpless when she had grown accustomed to seeing him confident, sure of himself, disdainful of any assistance. He wanted always to stand apart from the world and look at it from the outside, she said, while defying anybody to hurt him; so she didn't like to think of him being hurt and almost helpless. Timid, she glanced at

Hubert to see if he thought her notion of his brother a bit ridiculous; but he smiled, nodding his head vigorously, and said, "You're right, Marion. That's the trouble with him, but he'll be O.K."

For dinner the food was simple, abundant and not badly cooked; the steak, though, was fried too much. Mrs. Bousneau explained that they would have had more company if they had come two weeks earlier. Last week she had had two engineers from the Falls; to-morrow, an electrician, who was going to work on one of the gold properties, would be coming to stay with them. If the mines ever opened up again she would have a full house and make plenty of money, but the trouble was the gold mines had been wildcatted out of existence and there was too much sulphur in the iron ore to make heavy production worth while. The construction camp up at the Falls, where they were building the power house, was a little too far away to get many boarders from, and it was her tough luck that it was the only place in the country where there was any work. Men from all over the country came on the boats, on the trains, bumming or paying, to this one camp looking for work; they came from as far south as the Soo and as far north as James Bay, always looking for work and seldom finding it. The contractor at the Falls, McLean, a really nice man, gave them a meal when he couldn't give them work, and then they picked up their packsacks and hiked up to the junction looking for a box car going west.

"How do these people live here at the Mission?" Hubert asked.

"Don't be silly," the woman said, laughing. "Heh, Charlie," she said to her husband. "The young man wants to know what people at the Mission do for a living? You ought to know."

"Well, I got my team of horses," he said sheepishly.

"That's it. He's got his team of horses. I didn't think of it. Well, the others around here ain't got any horses and they go on living just the same. No one ever knows how the Indians live at the Mission. People have been asking that for years. No one ever worked but father and for some time father hasn't been able to get a job. Oh, they hunt a bit in the winter and they fish a bit in the summer, that's all, and they've been around here over a hundred years."

"Are they all Indians?"

"Well, I'd bet only wooden money on it. But they all collect the treaty money from the government. Over at the reservation, miles along the shore, there's a bunch of pure-blooded Indians who call these people here French, though everybody else calls them Indian. It's a bad question to ask," she said cheerfully. "Isn't there a little Indian in you, Charlie?" she asked.

"Not a drop," he said emphatically. "You can

bet your boots I'd be collecting treaty money if there was." But his eyes were brown, his hair was straight, and his cheek bones were high, though of course he had a little nose and a small mouth.

"I'm tired," Marion said. "I'm going upstairs and lie down."

"You call me if there's anything you want, darling," Mrs. Bousneau said.

Marion carried an oil lamp up to the small, clean room with the white bedspread. It got cool very early at night. Slowly she began to undress, thinking of nothing at all and feeling tired, but when she was almost naked, she put her hands over her breasts, remembering how long she seemed to have been waiting, and how she had thought all resisting would be over and she would have her lover in this country. Her body felt chilled. She got into bed and closed her eyes, feeling herself becoming one with the silence of the country. The night was so awfully still that she was too much aware of her own body, and was glad when she heard, faint and far away, the clang of iron being piled on iron over at the dock. "There's no use pretending," she thought. "I feel so disappointed." When she tried to express it so simply it seemed like a young girl's disappointment, and she smiled bitterly. Below were murmuring voices; Hubert would talk with Bousneau for hours. Peter was sleeping in the next room. For some reason she began to think sadly of her mother, who for years had gone on loving the dead officer, and she wondered if she was sitting alone in her room reading the evening papers. And just before she fell asleep she thought she heard the sound of Steve's boat as he turned the point, coming home.

15

ALL day they waited for the doctor who did not come. Peter lay flat on his back without moving. Hubert tried to be a nurse to him. Peter had insisted that Marion try and amuse herself outside, so she wouldn't spend all her time in the room. The two brothers amused each other. Hubert, who by this time had accepted the situation cheerfully, talked to Peter as if nothing had happened that could concern them in a serious way. Peter was also anxious to accept the situation, only he was afraid to move his back. He looked at his brother proudly and seemed ashamed of himself. There was no reason for being particularly proud of Hubert, except that he was sitting there by the bed talking happily about making a journey some day as far south as Merico. He wanted to see the old ruins in Yucatan, he said.

Then Peter said, "This must be pretty lousy up here for Marion. She expected such a great deal. It's not easy for her, anyway."

"Oh, don't worry so much about her."

"You have an awful lot of confidence in her, haven't you, Hubert?"

"Yes, I'd bet my eye-teeth on her. She's got guts and plenty of loyalty. You can't beat her."

"And in me, too?"

"Sure, Mike. I feel good about both of you. And besides, Marion is such a nice, swell-looking girl. She's so damned steady, that's what I wanted to say."

"What is she doing now?"

"A minute ago I could see her from the window. She was walking down to the water's edge, but she turned and went slowly up the hill to the dirt road by the bridge."

"I didn't know there was a bridge."

"There is anyway. Over the tributary river and the road from the dock up to the Falls passes over it."

"Then what did she do?"

"She was carrying a long stick in her hand and at the time she had no hat on. She was carrying a little beret in her hand."

"Did she seem cheerful?"

"When she passed the window she was whistling. She tried to talk with an idiot boy in a coat about eight sizes too large for him, and he grinned at her and hurried away, and so she laughed at him."

"That's good. The trouble about being here on your back is you think too much. I've been thinking about her mother, Mrs. Gibbons. I've been thinking about that big blonde, Patricia. I've been thinking how a woman like Mrs. Gibbons will long all her life for a simple love and get rubbed pretty steadily in the mud. Marion deserved a little luck up here. And I was thinking it might be better if something did happen to me, so it would let her out. It may be bad for her, as it is."

"Forget about the city. You're up in the country; isn't that what you wanted?"

"Yes, but all my thoughts are in the city."

"If you could look this place over you'd like it. What a country. The hills sweep on up to the summits. And what black rocks. Lord man, what a sea, and it's so hard and brilliant."

"Isn't that Marion coming up the stairs now?"

The door half opened and Marion put her head in the room. She was wearing a yellow sweater, fitting her tightly at the waist and showing her curving breast, a blue beret, far back on the side of her head, and a pair of riding breeks. In her hand she was carrying a long wand, taller than herself. Her head looked very small in the tight cap. Her lips were red, and her cheeks rouged. Such a costume seemed theatrically comic at the Mission. The Indian boy who had grinned at her so foolishly had hurried away to have a good laugh at her.

"No sign of a doctor yet, eh?" she said.

"He could hardly be here by this time, now could he?" Hubert replied.

She stood beside the bed. Bending down, she kissed Peter's lips with steady eagerness, forgetting all about Hubert, and her face was tense.

"How does it feel?" she said evenly.

"So swell. Please keep it up."

But she didn't want him to move his legs, so

she wiped the rouge off his lips with her handkerchief.

"Please keep it up," he said.

"Not now. Maybe to-night again. If you're good."

His lips seemed pale with the rouge wiped off.

"How does your back feel?" she said.

"Oh, my dear, you sound so competent and
practical."

"Please tell me, Peter. Don't tease me."

"It feels, when I'm lying still, as though a plasterer
had done a good job on me, and when I move my
legs I seem to feel the plaster breaking."

"Then if you don't move, I'll keep on sitting here."

This morning she seemed more cheerful as she
walked about the small room in her sandals, taking
short steps and looking at wide boards on the floor
which show the grain from so much scrubbing, then
looking up at the whitewashed ceiling, and at the
dresser, solid and simple, with the knob missing.
Her hair curled up from under her beret, and she
seemed even more of a woman in the breeks and
yellow sweater.

"What an elegant dresser," she said, looking with
admiration at the solid, simple frame. "I'd simply
love to have it. Don't you like it, Peter? Wouldn't
you like to buy it?"

"I haven't got any money."

"I wonder if Mrs. Bousneau would sell it to me.
But how would I get it out of here?"

"Oh, what an elegant figure you have," Peter said,

watching her eagerly. "If only I could get out of here."

"The better to love you with, my dear."

"And oh, what fine arms you have."

"The better to hold you with, my dear."

"And oh, what fine hips you have in those breeks, grandmother."

"The better—" she began, and then, glancing at Hubert, her face crimsoned and she turned away, saying, "Shame on you, Peter." She stood by the window, looking down intently at the freshly white-washed sill with weather cracks in the old wood, and the white lace curtains on the window.

"Are your thoughts on the market?" Peter asked, still looking at her.

"What am I offered?"

"A penny."

"Just a penny for such thoughts? Then you're no mind reader."

"Tuppence, then."

"Listen, my lad," Hubert said. "If this is a public auction I guess the old man can bid, eh?"

So for the rest of the morning the three of them were in the room, making jokes and trying to amuse each other, as if merely waiting for Peter to get up at any moment. Outside it rained lightly for an hour, raining out over the lake where the fine rain was like a thick gray mist. At noon time it cleared, and Marion and Hubert walked down by the water's edge to pitch stones at the surface weeds.

From what they had told him, Peter tried to have in his thoughts the whole world outside; he felt he knew the path that led to the main road going up to the Falls, Bousneau's team of horses, the foolish boy in the peak cap with the large old coat, and the pock-marked face of St. Leo, the storekeeper, who had failed three times, though his was the only store for miles around. St. Leo had failed because he charged too much for his canned goods and the village people had found out, in the course of time, that they could send down to the Soo and have food brought up on the steamer, for less than they paid to him. Each time he failed, St. Leo opened up a new store and reduced his prices; the freshly painted store with the false front had been open only a month and he was doing well. But, of course, as soon as he got the people trained to coming back to his store, he would begin to raise his prices and keep on till his customers remembered they could get food more cheaply from the Soo; then he would reduce the prices and wait for the customers to come back again. It was a simple process but St. Leo hadn't adjusted his sliding scale of prices properly.

Peter heard hardly any sounds of people talking, though there were over forty families at the Mission. The sun was very hot in the afternoon; they fished in the early morning and at twilight. A strong, brilliant afternoon sun withered and rotted the dilapidated plank dock, the old boat, picket fences and roofs caving and falling with age. Peter

wanted to retain this description of the village and
every time he heard a sound he tried to locate it in
the picture that was in his head. As he looked up
at the white ceiling, he wished he could hear sounds
from the dock, but he knew the men would
not begin loading again till evening. It was easier
to construct this small world in his mind than to go
on thinking of the city; and the only time he had
any downright pleasure in his thoughts was when he
had some notion about Hubert or Marion.

In the late afternoon Peter had a visitor. For a
moment they thought the doctor had come, as
Marion and Hubert, sitting together on the porch,
saw a young fellow in a blue English blazer coming
down from the dirt road to Bousneau's boarding
house. This fellow walked with the easy stride of a
young man who is accustomed to go ambling along
country roads and over meadows, and even from a
distance he was unlike the natives, who seemed to
walk lazily because of their awareness of the tre-
mendous distances, and the superiority of patience,
as a quality, rather than sprightliness. When the
eager young man saw Marion and Hubert on the
porch, he bowed politely and said he had heard, up
at the camp, that some one from the city was sick
at the boarding house. It had occurred to him
to pay a neighborly call. He lived in the Junction,
some forty miles away. As they went upstairs to see
Peter, this smooth-faced, fair-haired young man,
who looked remarkably clean in his gray, well-

pressed trousers and his blue blazer, explained that
his name was Richmond and he was the Anglican
clergyman for the district. At once the two brothers
and Marion began to talk rather formally and the
young man looked pained and unhappy, for he
wanted to be intimate with these city people; he
wanted to tell them the way he felt about the country. Hesitating at first, he intimated that he had
only been in the country two months. "Please sit
down, Mr. Richmond," Marion said.

With a cheerful smile, he said that he had left
England just two months ago and had come directly
to this country without even stopping overnight in
a city.

"Why the hurry?" Peter asked.

"In the seminary at home I looked at a map and
this country looked sufficiently unsettled and primitive and desolate to try me," he said simply.

"But you shouldn't have come here. It will kill
you," Marion said. "You should have stayed in the
city."

"The city is all right for old men of eighty," he
said scornfully. "I'll stick it, don't worry; I'll stick
it."

"Do you get many people to go to church up
here?"

"Oh, yes, we do very well," he said.

Peter, who was smiling and thinking the young
man splendid, asked if the Anglican Church was
doing well in England. "I read the foreign news,"

he explained. "I gathered there was some dissension among the Anglicans. Isn't the Anglo-Catholic movement growing stronger?"

"Why, yes, it is," Mr. Richmond said carefully.

"I was reading that the Anglican attitude to birth-control and so on may turn many over to Rome, eh?"

"There will never be any going over till the Romans accept Anglican orders," the young man said positively. Every time he used the word Roman, as he went on talking, Marion, just to amuse herself, used the word Catholic, till the fellow was piqued. He seemed to be watching his words carefully. They were talking about some notable converts to the Catholic Church, and the young man was so excited to be having such a conversation that his smooth, beardless face glowed with enthusiasm. For a moment he was silent and finally he said with the greatest diffidence, "I don't suppose you people are Catholics?"

"Marion is a Catholic," Peter said, smiling, "and we're—well, what are we, Hubert?"

Delighted, the young man drew his chair closer to the bed. "If you don't mind my saying something," he began, and looked around carefully. "I'm an Anglo-Catholic. But if the people around here knew I wasn't a straight Protestant, they wouldn't let me preach." Growing timid, he fumbled in his inner pocket and took out a small photograph which he handed around modestly; a picture of himself

in a soutane and wearing a beretta. He looked just
like a Catholic priest and he wanted them to see the
resemblance. He was delighted when they mentioned it. "In England they call me Father, just as
they do in the Roman community," he said, putting
the picture back in his pocket. He suggested that
they shouldn't mention the photograph to anybody.
"My mother sent it to me. I'm so glad to have you
people to talk to. I haven't had any kind of an intellectual conversation since I came here," he said.

Then Bousneau, who was writing a letter downstairs, called up, "Will one of you boys tell me how
to spell athletic?"

Hubert spelled the word slowly, while they
waited.

"Aren't there any Anglo-Catholics up here?"
Marion asked.

"Among the white people they don't know what
the word means," he said with disgust. "I have to
be the Protestant clergyman, and mind you, I agree
with Miss Gibbons that all Protestants are heretics.
How I hate the word."

Miss Gibbons, who was surprised, smiled as
the young man went on to explain that he didn't
despair; for example, the Indians and the French
around there were nearly all Catholic, but to amuse
himself the other day, he went over to an Indian
settlement and explained that he was an Anglican
who would like to say mass. The Indians were
enthusiastic at once, and an old woman got out a

sewing machine for an altar and put a table cloth over it. He said mass. "It was wonderful," he said. "Mind you, those Indians seemed to know the difference between an Anglo-Catholic and a Catholic and it pleased me a great deal." His theory was that in the old days some of the first missionaries must have been High-Anglicans, who converted the Indians, and then, later on, Catholic missionaries came and reconverted the High-Anglican Indians to Catholicism. It never seemed to occur to him that the Indians thought he was some one who wanted to say mass, and didn't care much anyway.

As he got up to go, he said anxiously, "May I come again? I don't get much of a chance to talk to people around here."

"By all means come any time," they said.

"Thanks a lot," he said, and from the window they watched him going up the path to the dirt road to wait for the truck to pass on the way up to the Falls. In his blue blazer and with his bare, very English, fair head and his well-pressed gray trousers, he looked as if he had just been following a boat race on the English Thames.

"Can you imagine a guy like that in this country?" Hubert said.

"He's splendid. I'm glad he came," Peter said softly.

"But could there be anything more ridiculous than that solitary Anglican in this wild country?" Hubert said.

"He's such a lovely boy, too," Marion said.

"He's splendid, I tell you."

"But he makes it all seem like an opera, a comic opera," she said slowly.

That evening at twilight, when Peter was alone, he lay very still, trying to get the feeling of the special quality of the country. The hours were long. A moon rose early. The room—the wall by the bed—was splashed with moonlight. He was aware of the dark, majestic, encroaching hush, and felt uneasy. At this time every night a big bull moose came out to the river a little way down the shore to drink and look out over the water. Peter wanted to have in him some of the strength of the loneliness of the country. He moved his legs slightly. "In this country there's no room for me as I am," he said.

But when Marion came into his room on tip-toe and sat beside him on the bed and he smelt the fragrance of her skin and hair, he felt in the dark for the neck of the blouse she was wearing and undid the ribbon. He untied the neck of her dress and kissed her small white breasts. And he didn't want her to go away or leave him at all that night.

16

A TRUCK on the way down to the dock the next day brought the doctor, an enormously fat man in a black coat and seven-gallon black hat, a vest straining at the buttons till his shirt beneath was revealed in a pattern that was a series of figure eights, and a hot red face requiring a good deal of mopping with an oversized handkerchief. Breathing deeply, then wheezing as though suffering from asthma, he went in to see Peter and placed his long black leather bag by the bedside. He sat down with his knees far apart. At one time he had done a very good business in the country but now a younger doctor, farther up the line at Franz, was able to get around more quickly. His examination of Peter was long, serious, hesitant and rather futile. At first he was flustered, then exasperated, then assertive like a man who didn't have a very good idea of what was actually bothering him. "If a hospital with an X-ray were here it would be simple," he said. He seemed anxious to give the impression that he was accustomed to running into hospitals three or four times in a morning before noon, when, in reality, he had hardly seen a hospital for fifteen years.

"There's a small fracture there," he said. "It may be serious. It got worse by your trying to walk around with it. A small piece of a vertebra was probably broken. It usually affects the legs. But it seems to be knitting now." He was honestly wondering whether he ought to have Peter moved to the dock, and then, on the steamer, to the city, or whether he ought to leave him there to rest without moving. "The trouble is," he said, "such a fracture is probably healing by now, and that may be the trouble. Can you move your legs, my boy?"

"I guess I could, but I don't like to try. I can move my feet, though."

"It might have been better to hold you steady with some kind of splints."

"No. Not now."

"I guess it wouldn't be much use now, but stay there and don't try and move, do you hear?"

"I haven't felt much like jumping around, Doctor."

"Good."

"How long will I be like this?"

Frowning, the doctor said simply, "I don't know. You might be able to move in a few weeks with some luck."

"Do you hear what he said, Marion? He said he doesn't know how long I'll be like this."

"He's giving you lots of time, so you'll be all right. Isn't that so, Doctor?"

"Why that's it, that's it," the doctor said, smiling and surprised that he hadn't put it in exactly those words. He picked up his battered black bag and

patted Peter on the shoulder. "Keep cheerful, son,"
he said. "Be good."

Marion followed the doctor downstairs and sat on
the porch with him while he waited for the truck to
come back from the dock: the driver would honk
the horn, then the doctor would hurry up the incline,
puffing and blowing, and sit on the front seat with
the driver and tell him all about the patient.
Marion sat beside him on the porch, listening to his
heavy breathing and looking closely at the trampled
yellow grass in front of the house. There was a very
small picket fence by the path, as if Bousneau were
proud of his grass and didn't want his neighbors
to walk on it. She heard Bousneau behind the
house, at the shed, talking to his team of horses,
and soon he came out to the wagon track, perched
perilously and monumentally on a slanting,
cock-eyed seat held up by two small sideboards on
the wagon. Flourishing a long gad and puffing vigorously at his corn-cob pipe, he said, "Geedap," and
headed the horses for the slope to the road; and
watching him, Marion thought idly that the horses
might stop suddenly and the wagon, without any
noise at all, would fall to pieces on the road in the
sunlight. . . . Of course it wouldn't matter. What
on earth did matter up here in this spectacular
country? she thought. She wondered if anything
that happened around there mattered at all to Steve,
who was so solitary in his bright sweater, so melancholy and so content. "The country is too vast.

We're too small," she thought. Almost indifferently she said to the doctor, who had just glanced at her and decided that she had the most remarkably clear skin he had ever seen on a woman, "I suppose he's hurt worse than it seems?"

"Not exactly, Miss Gibbons. I mean, he may get up and around all right, but he may never really get over it."

By her manner of speaking he never suspected that she had any deep interest in the young man.

"Will he be all right finally, do you think?"

"The spine is a very delicate piece of machinery. But it doesn't seem to be affecting his legs. I'm hoping he won't be really crippled but there's a bad chance he might limp, or move a leg awkwardly, or something like that, if you know what I mean."

"There's no danger of his being paralyzed?"

"I don't think so. Not now. I'd be more afraid of it twisting him a bit, see? But it's hard to say. You can see that."

"Oh, yes, I can see it," she said.

Her lips trembled, as if she were going to speak, but she closed her eyes. When she opened her eyes they were bleared by a mist. Blinking, she looked candidly at the doctor and had the feeling she had really seen him for the first time, an enormous, fat, honest, muddled man; she was saying to herself,

"Oh, my God. Peter a grotesque." If she cried out, her voice would be lost so easily, so pathetically in the great, wooded green valley. Inside her she held on tightly to this strong feeling, fearing that if she dared to express it there in the sunlight, it would become utterly unimportant; it was good to feel it hurting inside her. "He'll be crippled. There's no doubt about that," she kept on saying to herself. "He'll never be any good again. He'll be going around on a string." Looking down at a few square feet of soil by the edge of the porch, she saw two or three sprigs of sweetpeas, hardly above the ground, three pale pink flowers, so frail and delicate they seemed to assume a marvelous, sudden importance. They looked so gay. Mrs. Bousneau, who had planted the sweet peas as a joke, had forgotten about them.

The loud honking of a horn and the rattle of the truck coming up the road disturbed her. Picking up his bag, the doctor shook hands hastily and went wobbling up the path.

Hubert, wearing a V-necked brown sweater of Bousneau's, which fitted him nicely at his broad shoulders but hung in folds around his waist, came out on the porch and said, smiling cheerfully, "Let's take a walk, Marion."

"All right, where'll we go?"

"I haven't been along the road yet. I thought we might walk down it a piece."

"Suits me," she said.

Keeping in step, they walked up the path to the road. For a hundred yards, on the side of the road by the Mission there was a potato patch owned by

St. Leo, the storekeeper. Hubert talked casually about the possibility of growing wheat in this country, and seemed to have forgotten about the doctor's visit. Irritated, she looked at him. She could see the side of his face and his pipe sticking out of the corner of his mouth. He needed a shave, though the dark growth of hair looked good on him. She kept waiting for him to say something about his brother, but he went on to say that the potato crop would be good this year, and he had heard they were growing wheat farther up the line at Hearst. Of course, the country was flat up there, he said, near James Bay. "Hell's bells, what can you say to a boy like that," she thought, for by this time, in her own mind, she was absolutely certain that Peter would be crippled; it even seemed to be necessary to the pattern of her life to have it that way. Angrily she stared ahead. They were up the road, almost opposite the waterfall, where the water was white, foamy and bubbling in the sunlight, shady and dark with hardly a ripple on the surface of the pool below the Falls, and almost stagnant in the puddles at the rim by the boulders where water skeeters hopped on the surface.

"I wonder what the fishing would be like there," he said.

"Do you want to try it?"

"Not now. It's too bright now.

"Shall we turn and walk down? All right, come on."

"Nice fellow, the doctor," he said, as if he had enjoyed a social call from the man. "Of course he's a very stupid man, but he's a nice fellow just the same."

She had so much sudden resentment, she was afraid to answer him. At the moment she hated him. She wanted to hit him, hurt him, make him cry out and then feel good, watching his pain. The road, which had been cleared through the bush, was marked by deep wagon tracks. Pale, small blue flowers and wild ripe raspberries were along the road and they stopped to pick a handful of berries and eat them, but many had been ripening too long in the sun. Hubert, who had taken off his hat, was trying to fill it.

"What do you want them for?" she asked.

"Peter will go for these in a big way with cream."

For a moment she thought eagerly he was going to talk about his brother, but he went on picking the berries without stopping till they both noticed the small French Indian graveyard by the side of the road. For a hundred years the mission people had buried their dead in this plot that wasn't more than two hundred square feet. Around each grave was a small, unpainted, warped and twisted picket fence. One grave, which had been well preserved, had an iron screen around it to keep out the underbrush that steadily encroached, year after year, over the whole cemetery. There were some old inscriptions in French and English, and on some of the graves,

bunches of withered wildflowers were done up with
bits of faded ribbon that had rotted in the rain and
sun. Outside the little cemetery, indeed, on the
other side of the road, it was so far removed, was
one small fenced-in grave of a Protestant boy. No
one had ever been quite sure why he had become a
Protestant, but when he died, of course, they had to
bury him in another cemetery, which he had all to
himself. And below this cemetery, on the same side
of the road, was a solitary grave in unhallowed
ground; a suicide grave for a young man from the
Mission, who had, some said, been drowned in the
river by his own wish, but who, according to others,
had simply got drunk and had fallen in. Since no
one ever got drowned around there they took it for
granted he must have been a suicide.

"I like this. I think it's swell," he said. "Here's
the whole village for years, if they had only stuck
up a few tombstones."

"I don't see that it's so amusing," she said testily,
wanting to quarrel with him about something.

"Oh, it is, in its own way," he said, as if her objection was not to be taken seriously.

"Hubert," she said sharply, "for God's sake snap
out of it. Complacency can be carried to an extreme,
don't you think? I'm sure your tranquillity is
admirable, but so few people in the world can afford
it. And I don't see how you can, either, when you
don't know how it'll turn out with Peter."

"Peter? Why he'll be all right, Marion," he said, looking worried for the first time.

"He won't be all right, I tell you. He'll never be all right again. I know. I feel it. You don't."

"But I'm just as sure he will be, Marion."

"You don't feel anything. You're so smug. I'm fed up with you. Can't anything get under your skin? I'd like to shake it out of you. You make me hate you. Sure, you accept everything, don't you, sickness or in health and so on and so on and so on. You and your brother get together and seem to forget there's any one else in the world. And I know he'll be crippled. Wake up, do you hear?" she said breathlessly, the words having poured out of her.

He seemed deeply hurt, as he stared at her; not that he was worried about Peter, but because of her. For a moment he was so upset he appeared to be losing all his faith in her and, for the first time, he faltered and was unsure of himself. Then he turned and left her, and walked back along the road, his big body leaning forward as he carried in his hand the hat full of berries for Peter.

Marion sat down weakly on a stump by the road and was so sorry for herself she began to cry, for the thing she most wanted in the world seemed very far away from her; and then she jumped up and ran stumbling along the road, shouting, "Wait a minute. Wait a minute, Hubert. Oh, Hubert, just

a minute. I want to speak to you." She caught up
to him at the path going down to the Mission.

"I'm awfully sorry, honestly I am," she said, trying hard to get her breath, and pushing her fair
hair back behind her ears. Speaking in her soft,
husky voice she looked at him eagerly and linked
her arm under his, pulling him close to her, for she
knew she had hurt him. "I've got a real sadistic
streak in me, all right," she said wistfully.

"Oh, nonsense," he said. "You're really a fine little
guy, Marion."

"Oh, no, I'm not. I'm a selfish, impatient and
determined woman."

"No, you're okay with me, and always have been.
This business simply gets on your nerves a bit,
that's all."

"Well, please don't mention it to Peter, will you,
Hubert?"

"Why should I, if it's all right with me?"

"I know you feel rotten about it as well as I do,
only I seem to have been wanting him to live with
me for so long." And as she tried to smile, she felt
her cheeks getting hot.

So they went down the path arm in arm to the
boarding house, and on the way passed old Marie,
seventy-three years old, ninety per cent Indian, who
smiled toothlessly, and went by on her way down to
the dock, a walk of two miles. A tourist, very likely
some big fellow in fishing boots and leather jacket,
had decided to go into the woods trout fishing, and

wanting some one to look after him, had sent up to the Mission for old Marie with her long flowing skirts.

When Marion went into Peter's room, he said, "I heard you shouting to Hubert. What was the matter?" His face was white, though he was still trying to appear disdainful of his predicament.

"I was shouting to him from the hill."

"I thought you might have fallen in the river. I was worried for a minute."

"No. He had just sauntered away from me and I was trying to catch up to him."

"I see. Say, the doctor wasn't very confident, was he? Maybe I'll be stuck here awhile. That'll be tough, won't it?"

"How do you feel now, Peter, boy?"

"About the same. It's easier not moving. But why don't you go ahead and have some fun? Why don't you and Hubert go trolling. Get that fellow Steve to go with you."

"We will to-morrow, if you want us to."

Tenderly she bent down and whispered. "I'd do anything on earth for you, you know that, don't you, Peter?" She brushed her cheeks against his. But then she felt frightened and put her arms around him, trying to hold on to him as though she could feel him slipping away from her.

"Why, what's the matter, dear? I can see you blinking your eyes?" he said.

"Nothing's the matter. Nothing at all."

"Were you wasting your time feeling sorry for me?"

"Not really. And not really sorry for myself either. Did you ever look up suddenly and see the sun shining on the summit of a snow-tipped mountain, and want awfully hard to reach it?"

"No, I didn't."

"Well, for that matter neither did I," she said laughing, and as Hubert came into the room, she said, "Hubert's the only one who has climbed his own mountain, aren't you, Hubert?"

"You bet your boots," he said emphatically.

"Tell us what you've been thinking about, lying there," she said to Peter.

Frankly, he said that first of all he had thought it would be horrible to be inanimate from the waist down, and possibly think all day of women; and for some reason, after that thought, he had wanted to write a letter to his father; a few days ago he had started a letter to his father but hadn't finished it. And then he had thought for a long time of Marion, he said, and he had wondered if she were having the same thoughts about him when she was alone. About that time he heard Bousneau talking to the electrician, who had arrived and was going up to the mine at once, to see some new machinery. He had listened to them talking and then his thoughts had drifted till he remembered a street walker he had once known, who wanted to own a millinery shop and make smart, neat little hats, and he had decided that if he ever got a lot of money he would buy a store for her, and let her amuse herself making the neatest little hats, though he knew she would probably still sell herself more often than she sold the hats. That had made him think about the noise in the city, the noise that drove people insane and filled the asylums, and yet he had admitted to himself the futility of trying to escape into the woods. "Whatever is to be done culturally, creatively, economically will all be done in the city. Whatever is to rise up from the ashes of the old American world will have its growth in the city," he said. "That's what I was thinking when Hubert left you and you called to him, Marion."

"Isn't it funny," she said, "the way we keep on talking about the city when we were so eager to get away from it?"

"Maybe it is," he said, "but outside of you, there doesn't seem to be much to think about. There's nothing else for me to do but go on thinking. And from up here you can get the city under your eyes. You know what I was thinking? I was thinking it would seem so good to walk through the residential districts and see the rows of trim, tidy green lawns, and the wide smooth roads, or in some other part of the city downtown, see the restaurant windows with the beef roasting in them and the crowds pushing in. Maybe I can't appreciate from here how grand this country is with the rocks and the lake and the hills. When you're on your back you like to be in your

own country. You know what I'd like? I'd love to
see a newspaper every morning. I wonder what's
going on in Russia. Oughtn't the world series to be
starting about now, Hubert? I guess it looks like
the Athletics to win again, eh?"

Marion was only half listening. She was thinking how, earlier in the day, she had been listening for bird songs, and then, so very distinctly,
among the chirping of many birds, she had heard
the sublime warble of the purple finch: breathless,
she had gone down from the steps and walked
quietly over to the tree: the bird wasn't up among
the leaves: it was sitting only a few feet away from
her, small, pale purple and delicate: she had been
delighted to see it so clearly. While Peter went on
talking about the city, she was still thinking of the
flowing warble. Hubert didn't interrupt his brother.
He was letting him talk himself out. Finally Peter
began to twitch, and they knew he ought to be
sleeping.

After dark Marion was sitting on the porch by
herself, thinking of her mother, when she heard the
twanging of a guitar in St. Leo's store. She heard
a woman's sudden laughter, and the roistering laugh
of a man. Hesitant, she stood up, feeling eager for
excitement, and walked out to the moonlit path.
The moonlight was shining on the wide smooth
waters in the valley, throwing silver sashes across
the dark velvet water. It was so bright, quiet, cloud-
less and intensely clear, she could hardly see the

stars. Just to disturb the stillness she bent down and picked up a small stone her toe had touched and tossed it down the bank to the water and listened for the plopping splash. The dark bush on the hills seemed to hang over the Mission. She walked toward the lights in the store. The door was open. She crossed the shaft of light and went in. From the back of the store came the sound of laughing and shouting. As she went into the store, her hands were in the pockets of her breeks and she looked around coolly, twitching the corners of her mouth. Light from the lantern, hanging from a ceiling hook, shone on her smooth blonde head. Two workers from the Falls were sitting on an upturned soap box with a Mission girl. They had come down with some liquor. On another box, an expressionless half-breed was sitting, patiently twanging an old guitar. One of the Falls men, a red-faced, heavy-set, good-natured young Scotchman, was a carpenter; the other, a pock-marked, swarthy man in a khaki shirt, was a truck driver. They were taking turns pouring glasses of whiskey into the girl, who squealed, twisted, giggled, squirmed, and embraced them passionately. The light shone on her faded blue coat, on her straight black hair, and her large, very white teeth. With sneering hostility, she glanced at Marion and shrugged her shoulders. She was good-looking, but her face was expressionless. Her eyes snapped brightly and she kept rubbing her tongue around her shining new store teeth.

"Hello," Marion said. "Would you like to give me a drink?"

"Surest thing you know, baby," the Scotchman said eagerly as he poured her a good stiff shot from the half-empty bottle. She took half of it at a gulp very smoothly. Then she smiled. For a moment, the half-breed, who was strumming the guitar, glanced at her thoughtfully, and continued his methodical twanging. Marion smiled at the dark girl to show that she wanted to become one with her for the evening and with a quick gulp she took the rest of her whiskey and sat down beside the red-faced Scotchman. Hardly able to believe his good luck, the Scotchman put his woollen-sleeved arm around her, squeezing her ardently. The other man tickled the dark girl till she squealed and nearly lost her teeth.

Then they heard boots scraping on the veranda and Hubert came through to the back of the store. When he saw Marion, the blood went out of his face and he had nothing to say at all. They asked him to have a drink. "Sure, I'll take a shot," he said. And shaken, he sat down.

The dark girl, who had become remarkably hilarious, began to sway her hips and sing a song in French that had a refrain, *Couchez avec Rosi*. They all learned that one line and shouted it heartily. *Couchez avec Rosi*. Marion had a deep contralto. Hubert began to enjoy himself and thought, lightheartedly, that Marion was merely being a good fellow.

At last, Marion put her hand out to Hubert, and after kidding the others, and leaving them in good humor, they went out. Outside on the path, going along to the boarding house, Marion said, "I wouldn't have minded five or six good shots, but they didn't have enough to go around and they have the night ahead of them." As she felt herself expanding, then contracting, she felt irritably that Hubert was standing apart from her. "Maybe it's the liquor in me," she thought, and smiled at him.

But when she was alone in her own bed she thought with warm excitement of the good time she had been having in the store.

17

BUT then she grew ashamed of herself. She became calm and patient and desperately eager to be happy. She waited on Peter and delighted in doing all the little things for him. She lit his cigarettes; she brought him food. Sometimes he wanted to get up and clean himself, but she insisted on washing his hands and face for him. She washed his arms and put her cheek against the hair on his chest, and she rubbed his skin with a heavy rough towel till it glowed ruddily. Then she combed his hair and, to amuse herself, parted it in the middle and made two spit curls on his forehead, and then hurried to get her hand mirror so he could see what he looked like. Laughing, he rumpled his hair all over his head. She grew sober, looking at him, and bending down, told him to hang on to her tightly and press his head against her breast. Day after day she tried to find new little things to do, but soon in the small white room she found herself doing the same things over and over again.

It was hardest of all for her when she was with him at night, for then they knew they were both wanting the same thing. They were motionless beside each other, thinking always of loving each other. Sometimes the nights were so quiet when the moon was full that it was silly to pretend to be very gay when she was crouched beside him, and in such a time their eagerness and longing for each other seemed even stronger as she whispered steadily and jerkily a few slow words. He muttered sometimes as he shifted restlessly, "When I get a bit better I'll love you so much you'll wither and die. The things we'll do when I'm better." It was always a half pleading whisper, "When I'm better." He couldn't seem to get used to having his back hurt him when he moved it. Every morning he said, "I'll be up soon." Brushing her hair against his face she whispered, "Wait, wait. Wait."

In the mornings, when the sun was shining so brilliantly on the white-capped waves far over the lake, and she could see the river water running so clearly and smoothly, it was much easier for her to be gay. In the daylight she was able to look for things to amuse them and be full of teasing and cheerful laughter.

One afternoon she was with Steve and Hubert down by the point between the lake and the bank at the mouth of the river. Steve was showing her how to make a fire by using a few pieces of wood. He got two flat pieces of cedar, and a short slender piece with rounded ends. He clamped the slender piece upright between the two flat pieces of cedar, but first of all he had taken a bow and looped the string around the upright stick. As he worked the bow back and forth like a saw, the upright stick that he clamped down with his other hand on the flat cedar kept on spinning hotly. It made an indentation on the soft cedar. First a faint spiral of thin blue smoke went up from the browning indentation, then there was the smell of burning wood. A little pile of cedar dust accumulated around the spinning upright. Marion, who was down on her hands and knees with her face close to the bow, said eagerly, "Why doesn't it flame now you're making the sparks?"

"There's a kind of punk that grows on birch trees. I'll show it to you some day," Steve said. "The Indians have it all dried out; they make the spark, blow on it and let it get at the dried punk. Once it gets lighted you can't put it out. It's always smouldering." Laughing, he went to throw the sticks of cedar and the bow away, but Marion said, "No, no, no, I want them." Taking them in her hand and looking pleased with herself, she asked to be rowed back to the boarding house.

Swaggering into Peter's room with a hand on her hip, she said laconically with a kind of professional ease, "Hello, sweetheart, like to see me make a little fire?"

"What have you been doing with those sticks?" he said.

"Fire without matches for you, sweetheart, and look. Nothing up the sleeves, no rabbits in the hat, no wires, just the sticks, now watch me," she said as she got down on her knees on the floor. Delighted with herself, but anxious to appear competent, she adjusted the bow and the upright stick, clamped the upright between the two flat pieces of cedar and began to work the bow industriously, saying nothing, absorbed and serious. When the first wisp of smoke appeared her face was wreathed in smiles of pleasure as she looked up proudly at Peter. Then she tightened the bow and kept on working lustily while she smiled at him; it was only a thin bow and the string was now too tight; the wood snapped. "Oh, dear," she said. "There wasn't even a spark." She kept on looking at the broken bow and the two sticks in her hand, "Oh, gee, just imagine," she said, and looked at Peter as though she were going to cry. "I wanted to show you how to do it," she said.

"Never mind dear, I saw how it was done."

"No, you didn't. And besides, we might get shipwrecked some time, or lost at the North Pole, and then what would we do if we couldn't make fire?" she said.

"I'll have to learn to make fire then, so we'll be warm in the winter," he said, as she bent her head down beside him. He started to kiss her hair and smell it, and then kiss her eyes, to console her as though she were a very little girl. Brightening a bit, but keeping her head down beside him, she said, "All right, I'll tell you about it then. You make a spark, see. There's a kind of punk that grows on birch trees and it lights easily when it dries and then it smoulders and you can't put it out. I'll show it to you some day."

"And where did you learn all this?"

"Steve showed us, down by the lake."

"Do you like him?"

"I admire him rather than like him. He seems to be the kind of a man who never wonders whether anybody likes him or not, any more than he wonders whether the country likes him. But he seems so dreadfully competent."

"He must seem mighty competent compared with me right now," Peter said, twisting his mouth at the corners.

"But you don't seem to realize, Peter, that it doesn't make me unhappy any longer to see you lying there. I want to do everything for you. I want to be so very competent. I love looking after you. Look at me. Don't I look happy? Did you ever see such a ridiculously happy damsel? But I can't seem to find enough little things to do for you. All the little things seem to dry up so quickly."

All day long she hunted outside for things that would amuse or interest him. She brought him shells from the beach, blue wildflowers from the hills, her hat full of blueberries, some medicinal herbs, a wide flat leaf that grew abundantly on the hills and was good for wounds, a piece of hematite, the iron-bearing rock, birch bark, small boughs of balsam, spruce and cedar. She seemed to be trying to bring everything that was outside into the small white room. She was really so eager that Peter sometimes looked at her uneasily, wondering whether she was measuring off her courage against her disappointment. Every time she returned to the room, he looked up, trying to catch some fleeting expression of discontent on her face. But she was so bright and cheerful he couldn't help smiling as though he could hardly believe his good luck in having such a girl. Very approving, he lay on the bed with his hair combed so nicely and his head looking large and smooth on the white pillow, and he tried to conceal his inward happiness by making many casual realistic remarks. But his blue eyes, which were bright with love for her, followed her wherever she moved in the room, and when she was outside, he listened for the faintest noises that would tell where she was and what she was doing. He never tired of talking to his brother about his girl. Even when they were making a conversation about far-away places like Mexico or Russia, or talking about the customs of the Ojibway Indians that lived along the lake, or the glimpse of a big moose drinking by night at the river, he was apt to start talking about Marion. Her gentleness completely delighted both of them. When she came into the room and interrupted them, they looked up at her, saying nothing and smiling.

Early in the morning she and Hubert went down to the extreme black rock tip of the point to cast for pickerel at the mouth of the river. Hubert, who had a fancy striped bathing suit under his trousers, had been casting for only a few minutes when his spoon got caught far out on the ledge of a submerged rock.

The length of his line was out and he couldn't get the spoon off the rock. Marion held the rod while he slipped off his trousers and swam out. She saw him dive. When he came up, he shook his head and swam back to the shore: there was an undercurrent from the river, and sand at the bottom like quicksand: he had sunk down and thought he would never get up. He still wanted to get the spoon. With Marion he went walking around the point on the lake side, looking for some one, and they were both astonished to see an old red-shirted Indian and a small boy in a battered canoe. They were from the reserve along the lake and they had been picking blueberries on the hills. Three big pails of blueberries were in the bottom of the canoe. The old Indian was bundled up in his heavy shirt as though it were a cold fall day. "They're just the guys for me," Hubert said, running down to the water and waving his arms. "Heh," he called. "Would you mind doing me a good turn? My line is caught on the rocks, just off the point. I was wondering if you would paddle around there and unhook it from the canoe, if you don't mind." He was very polite as he stood there in his neat fancy city bathing suit, smiling and eager. The old Indian, looking at him blankly, shrugged his shoulders. The Indian boy smirked and put his hand over his mouth. "Would you mind?" Hubert repeated. Looking at him contemptuously the old Indian began to paddle away, and when they were a little way out from the shore, the old fellow smirked at the boy, who hadn't stopped grinning from the time he had first seen Hubert. "I wonder what's so funny about me?" Hubert said uneasily to Marion. He was so friendly and amiable himself, he couldn't understand why anybody should be so rude.

This was all something for Marion to describe for Peter. First she mimicked Hubert's puzzled, hurt expression, then she mimicked the contemptuous, indifferent expression of the old Indian and the smirk of the boy. She seemed to have caught every gesture and movement. The brothers, who did not know she had such a talent for mimicry, kept on looking at each other and applauding her enthusiastically.

But the finest time of all was the night when she and Hubert were sitting down on the jagged rocks by the lake not far away from the wide mouth of the river. They were watching the night coming on. There was hardly any movement among the leaves on the trees in the clump behind them. They had been talking about Eugene O'Neil, wondering whether *Anna Christie* was his best play, and the conversation had trailed away till they were silent. Far down the shoreline the sky was crimson. There were no clouds at all. Night came on. A loon cried mournfully. The vast smooth water became slate gray, then the sky became slate gray, till the horizon faded and there was no line between the sky and the water. All the rest of the world seemed to have

slipped down behind the vanishing skyline. They
were high up in the deep silence. She was a bit
afraid. It was like watching the night come on for
the first time in a new world. Then came one western shining star, then a handful of stars, and the
towering rocks on the shoreline loomed up dark
and close till they, too, were lost in the starlight.
Only the great lapping lake waters soothed the
rugged shore. It was soon full night. As the northern
lights began to sweep vastly across the sky, she felt
a strange harmony and peace all around her, and
she felt herself groping toward it and trying to become a part of it. She felt, as her heart began to
beat heavily, that her love for Peter was the way
toward a more complete and final peace than any
she had ever known, and that they might both know
the mystery that rounded out the night. "Let's go,"
she said abruptly to Hubert as she took his hand,
and they climbed back over the rocks and through
the clump of trees heading for the river. Just as
they came out of the trees to the bank of the river,
she saw the moonlight for the first time. They
walked suddenly out into the moonlight gleaming
on the sandy bank and silvering all the wide mouth
of the river. Out beyond the mouth, in the lake, the
long sandbar gleamed whitely.

"Row me back, hurry," she said, almost breathless.

As they went up the wide river slowly with only
the sound of the oarlocks on the dark deep water,
and the hills hanging up around them in the great

valley, Hubert said, "It isn't much like the city, is it?"

"No."

She kept looking up toward the Mission at the little white boarding house in the short row of tiny houses on the bank, and sometimes she looked up impatiently as though to say to Hubert, "Hurry, hurry." She was holding on to a feeling within her that she wanted to share with Peter, but which was becoming almost too big for her.

As soon as the boat touched the old rotting wharf, she jumped out ahead of Hubert, scrambled up the bank in the sand and ran into the boarding house and up to Peter's room. Standing by the door, she hesitated, looking at his face which she could see so clearly in the moonlight.

"I heard you coming," he said quietly. "I heard you hurrying."

"Peter, I wanted to run. It was so beautiful. There was something I wanted to come in and share with you. We were sitting down by the lake. The way the moon shone so suddenly. We couldn't see it by the lake. We just walked into it."

"It was shining in here too, by the window," he said.

"But you had to think about it."

"No. At first I was lying here thinking as soon as I was back in the city I'd go and see this new game of box lacrosse they say is faster than hockey, and then I just stopped thinking."

"It got monotonous?"

"Not to-night. Not to-night at all, for some reason. Other times it has, but to-night it was very calm and peaceful lying here."

Sitting down on the bed beside him, she said, "Peter, I'm so happy. I'm so very happy. Don't you believe me?"

"Dear girl, what's the matter? You're going to cry."

"No I'm not. I'm fine. But to-night, it's just like it ought to be always. Peter, it's turning out up here just as I wanted it to. I felt so fine down there by the lake. It's just as it ought to be."

"Not quite," he said, shifting his body and twisting his mouth wryly.

"Oh, I know, I know, and I feel how the pain hurts you. But now I want to wait, and I want to always need you."

She lay down on the bed beside him and her hand caressed his face. He kissed her four times on the mouth. She curled herself up on the bed beside him, and remained mute and still. Downstairs Hubert was talking to Bousneau. She remained there beside him, holding his arm contentedly but tightly, and the moonlight, which had been streaming across the floor of the room, moved over to the corner, then up the wall, and at last it was dark in the room.

18

THE doctor came again. Peter looked at him anxiously and made the deprecating motion with his hand. The doctor's bulging red double chin was dropping down over his collar as he leaned over the bed. Wheezing and snuffing and making deep guttural noises to himself, he tried to find many things to do to prolong the examination so he would have more time to come to a decision. When he jerked his body upright, Marion was sure his vest buttons would snap off and fly across the room, yet she smiled, for he was making no pretense of professional competence. He was simply a worried country doctor who wished that a more plausible fellow practitioner had been there to give him advice.

"I didn't expect any noticeable change," he said at last.

"Then he's not worse?" Marion asked.

"I can't see that he's any worse."

"Would you be able to tell, just looking at him like that?" Hubert asked.

"No. I've got to admit you can't tell much. I can't feel much either," he said, shaking his head and looking more worried and ashamed of himself. "I never had a case like this up here requiring an X-ray. How do you feel, young man?"

"Just about the same, Doctor. Waiting, that's all."

"Would you think of going back to the city? Down to the Soo on the next boat, maybe, eh?"

"Lord, no. Not if I can help it," Peter said. "I'd like to stay here if I'm coming along at all. I'll be tap-dancing in a couple of days, Doctor."

"Oh, sure you will. That's the spirit," he said.

Hubert and Marion followed the doctor downstairs and when they were outside, Hubert said, "You were trying to tell him, Doctor, that he ought to go back to the city on the next boat, weren't you?"

"I meant that he ought to be X-rayed," the doctor said. "It's hard for anybody to say what's happened to his spine. I tell you frankly I'd hate to take the responsibility of leaving him here."

"Then you want him to be X-rayed," Marion said, leaning forward.

"He ought to be. But then I don't know but what it might do a lot of harm moving him. It's a predicament. It's got me puzzled." Taking off his big hat, he rubbed his cropped gray head with his knuckles. "It's up to you," he said. "Whatever you want. You see how it is."

"If you think he'd be just as well here," Marion began.

"I said I thought he ought to be X-rayed," the doctor interrupted. "Only I'd hate to advise that he be moved. Do you see what I mean? Maybe we'd better wait."

They stood on the porch, watching the doctor's big, wide body swaying heavily from side to side as he went along the path to the road. He walked with a stiff movement of his trunk-like legs. His trousers seemed immense. All of a sudden Marion began to run up the path after him, calling, "Doctor, just a minute." And when he turned, and she caught up to him, she said, "You really mean I ought to take him back on the next boat, don't you?"

"He ought to be X-rayed. That's what I mean. But if you want to leave him here, I'll look after him as best I can." The honest, good-natured man seemed to understand that she wanted to remain in the country. "I'll just leave it to you," he said. When he saw her looking frightened, he began to rub his boot sole on a small stone in the path. "I wanted to stay here," she admitted, "but now I don't know what to do. I'm afraid to move him." They were looking down at the ground, both silent, sharing a deep perplexity. Clenching her fists, she felt she was trying to hold on to a happiness that she had just touched and was rightfully hers. "Good-by, Doctor," she said. Frowning, the doctor shook his head, but he was relieved that she had made some kind of decision.

But when she returned to Peter's room she felt

weary and discontented. Standing by the window she looked at the hills like great cones with vast wooded slopes, bare in patches where there had been a fire, and with the sunlight gleaming on bare, dry boughs. They were all waiting. Peter, who was lying very still, hardly even moving his hands, felt some of the uneasiness that was inside Marion, as he watched her standing by the window.

"I can't make anything out of your smile," he said to her. "What do you think of when you look out the window?"

"I see the hills," she said.

"And what do they make you think of, Marion?"

"They make me feel small and unimportant, they're so rugged, hard and brilliant. My notions of people and things become unimportant. What is right, what is wrong, what is important, or any ambition, all seem unimportant here."

"Is there no answer at all to it?"

"There must be. I'm sure there is, but I can't figure it out."

"Did you say that nothing at all was important?"

"I meant the thoughts we cling to that worry us; they seem so small."

"Isn't it just the ideas we've been living by that suddenly seem to become unimportant up here?" he asked eagerly. "You know what I've been thinking? Last night I was wondering if you might make a mistake about this country, Marion. I was thinking that if I could be high up here in these hills looking closely at everything, wouldn't it be just our old way of thinking that would become trivial? Would it seem important for very long that I had always been a liberal instead of a conservative, or a communist instead of a socialist? Yesterday afternoon a small purplish bird must have been perched on the window sill and I could just see one of its wings in the sunlight. For a long time I did nothing but stare at the bird's wing, and then I thought how I might lift a dripping speckled trout out of a stream and look for a long time at it, too, or at the bark of a birch tree, or a chipmunk on its hind legs by a path, so then I suddenly looked for a long time at my own hand as if I had never seen it before, and I thought something inside me or you might go leaping up with a kind of ecstacy trying to get close to everything for the first time. A fellow like myself who has talked so much about the rights of the individual in a democratic society finds it terribly awkward even to think of the soul . . . I mean up here, even if you're forced clear of all the old notions you've lived by, you might even be steadier just being, well, just being. . . . There's no use going on," he said, smiling, "because I admit every time I get dull I long for the city instead of having such thoughts."

"I can't figure it out," she said. "There might be something even bigger underneath, but nothing of any accepted importance seems to count at all."

When she turned, his face was away from her by

the wall, and she knew she had hurt him. Smiling awkwardly, she said, "Peter, you're the only thing that matters to me. Don't let my silly bromides upset you. I know you're the only thing that matters to me. You can see that, can't you? And I know it." Out of contrition and loyalty she was speaking tenderly.

The next morning, with Steve and Hubert, she went trolling on the lake. They borrowed Bousneau's lines, and his hooks which were covered with white feathers and slender pieces of red cloth to attract the fish. Steve rowed the boat evenly, tirelessly, off that two-mile sandy beach, and Hubert and Marion had their lines out. There was one small island just off the end of the beach, and as they rounded it, there was a tugging on Hubert's line and he landed easily a small salmon trout. He landed it in the boat and had to hold it with his hand while he killed it. They went all the way back the two miles the length of the beach without catching anything, till they turned and came back by the small island. Where the beach ended, the hills began, the hills quickly becoming granite-faced, towering cliffs, very dark at the base, shooting straight up to the blue sky, and close by the cliffs, and the little island, the water was deep, shadowed, metallic and gleaming. Here Marion landed a lake trout, and within a minute Hubert landed a big fellow. They had caught the three fish at the one point in the water. "It's like pulling them out with your hand, here," Hubert said.

But Steve, who was looking out over the water, had seen small whitecaps far out in the sunlight and he shook his head. "The water changes very quickly on this old lake," he said. "Better not row back now. It's going to get rough. We'll land on the beach and wait. There's a trout stream up in there."

"We've only got a rod for bait casting," Hubert said.

"We could catch some grasshoppers on the beach," Steve said.

So they beached the boat. Steve dug a deep hole by a rock; he took a newspaper from the boat and wrapped three gleaming fish in it and put the parcel in the hole where the sand was damp and cool, then he filled the hole.

For half an hour the three of them wandered over the beach, over the litter of dried-up sticks and gray logs, over the hot sand in the sunlight, bending down, trying to catch grasshoppers that click-clicked away from them. You simply had to catch them with your hand. Marion was exasperated and Hubert was too, that they had such a hard time catching even the little ones, while Steve, hardly, moving from the one spot, was filling his hat with them.

Then they went into the woods, following the stream to a trout pool. Rapidly and surely, Steve went ahead on the narrow trail over fallen stumps and across rivulets till they could see only his golden-striped sweater through the trees. He waited to show them the tracks of a moose in swampy soil. Once he stopped beside a tiny pool by a little water-fall and pointed to a wild duck swimming in a circle, but they couldn't even see it. He went down to the pool. Thick branches were like a screen overhead at the pool, and they watched Steve go down on his knees, crawling silently from rock to rock, the move-ments of his body balanced and controlled, his face eager. He caught the duck with his hands. He laughed at it when it tried to dig its beak into his wrist. "Too small and out of season for eating," he said, but he carried the duck in his hands along the trail till the bush opened into a wide, still pond. He flung the duck at the water. Whirling in the air, to feel its wings, it dived sharply and heavily and did not stick its bill above the surface till it was full forty yards away by the other side of the pond. Marion, looking quickly at Steve, liked him for being so graceful, intelligent and contented.

They had to go on ahead, but the trail led only into the pond. Around the pond rim the underbrush was tangled and heavy with rotting logs drooping in the weedy water, and vines and grasses grayish, old and mud-covered where the water rose after the heavy rains. "We cross through the pond. It's not deep," Steve said. "I'll help you, Miss." Taking Marion firmly in his arms and holding her easily, he went wading out in the water. For a moment Hubert hesitated, then he followed them, and when he got accustomed to the water, he began to smile. Marion, with her lips twitching, glanced at Steve, who was looking straight ahead. Closing her eyes she liked feeling how safe she was and how surely he moved. His arms never sagged. His fingers weren't even digging into her. Then she felt his feet slipping on the mud, and opening her eyes, and feeling frightened, she put her arms tightly around his neck. "Nearly went that time," he said, smiling. Suddenly she said, "Put me down. I might as well get used to it." Even while he hesitated, she knew that he thought she ought to be wading in the water in her ordinary clothes, though it was up to her waist. He let her sink into the water, heard her gasp as her thighs felt chilled, and then he smiled openly and warmly when she started to follow Hubert. Her face was white. But when her flesh got used to feeling the wet heavy clothes, she felt exhilarated and liked it till she was almost at the end of the pond and had to wade through mud that was three feet deep. After that, whenever the trail was too narrow or difficult, they left it and waded up the stream. They could hear the sound of falling water. At a turn in the stream they came in sight of water falling narrowly over boulders eighteen feet high. At the top of the boulders, above the falls, was one deep little pool with foaming water, and Hubert said, "Just a minute, there ought to be something in there." He put a piece of grasshopper on a worm hook, and using his short steel rod, he kept on flicking at the pool in the rocks. First he was alert, then he grinned, then he was serious, then he grinned again. "There must be a big fellow or two in there," he said. "You two go on up where you're going. I'll stay here." They left him kneeling on the great rock, peering down at the pool.

Steve and Marion went farther up the stream to a place where three shallow pools were joined by short necks of water. The pools' surface was placid, the water hardly moving. "It may not look like a trout pool, but here it is," Steve said. Out in the pool, almost at the center, was a long, flat, dry rock. Before they waded out to it, Steve tore many bits of green brush from the trees, mostly from the balsam and spruce trees, till he had a big bundle under his arm. As soon as they stood on the flat rock, he made a pile of the green brush and placed it where the smoke would blow over their heads when he lit it, and Marion, watching him, was already slapping her ears, for the first blackflies were coming. A swarm of them followed. Then the smudge was lit and the heavy, rancid smoke blew overhead and the flies were scattered. "You keep the smudge going," Steve said to Marion as he adjusted the grasshopper bait on a hook. He was using a short steel rod like Hubert's. The line licked out over the water, dipping on one side, flicking neatly on another side of the rock, while Steve watched. The line stiffened and sunlight from the bit of blue sky above glinted on the squirming trout as it was lifted out of the water. As its eight inches were laid on the rock the sunlight sparkled on its speckled body. "The pool's full of them. Look over there. One just leaped out of the water." Marion had to look quickly to see them coming up at all. They fished that pool for an hour and a half and got six good ones. There were also five little ones about four inches long but Steve threw these back in the water.

Back at the waterfall where they had left Hubert, they saw him sitting in the sunlight, slapping his arms and neck. On the rock, beside him, was a single beauty of a speckled fellow almost a foot long, and looking, against the dull rock, like some magnificent gleaming crystal. Though Hubert's neck was badly bitten by the blackflies, he was smiling serenely, he seemed utterly happy. "It took me an hour to get that beauty and I'm satisfied," he said, feeling the little clots of blood hardening on his neck. Steve grinned at him.

Going down the trail, on the way back to the lake, Marion said to Steve, "You were going to show us that stuff like punk that grows on birch trees. The Indians use it for keeping a fire going."

He left them at once and darted out among the great trees, peering high up on one white birch after another, and finally he called, "Here." He pointed to something black and spongy near the crotch of the tree. "You cut that down and let it dry, that's it," he said.

"Thanks, Steve," she said, friendly and smiling.

On the beach they built a fire between two logs, one end laid over the end of the other log, and both pointing toward the lake to get the draft. "We'll eat some of the brook trout now and take the rest home, eh?" Hubert said. The pink flesh of the trout fried brown and crisp and tasted sweet, fresh and clean. By this time there were no whitecaps on the water, and hardly any breeze. While Hubert dug up the lake trout from the hold by the cool rocks, Steve cleaned the pans in gravel and sand, and the knives and forks, too, and buried all the refuse. The fire was put out carefully.

On the way home Hubert insisted on rowing. He splashed his oars, though he didn't row badly. There was fish for dinner for the Bousneaus and a feed of brook trout for Peter, who kept on questioning them till he had every incident of the trip clearly in his mind.

That evening she was on the sand beach for a while with Hubert. To amuse herself, she borrowed Hubert's knife and started to make chips of wood so she could light a fire without using paper, just as Steve had done. On her knees in the sand, she put the chips between the short logs for the draft, lit them and kept blowing on them. She heaped a handful of twigs on the tiny flame and smothered it so that the smoke went into her eyes and down her throat till she began to cough. Hubert, who was smoking his pipe and sitting a few feet away, tossing pebbles idly at the water, got up and wanted to

light the fire for her, but she would not let him near
it. As she whittled more shavings, she began to
think of Steve, and she leaned forward on her knees.
What did she actually know about him? she asked
herself. Why couldn't she treat him as she might
treat Bousneau? Maybe his deep calmness only concealed a lack of emotion; yet there was the soften-
ing in his eyes and the pity that first day when
Peter, climbing the bank, fell forward on his face,
and Steve had helped to carry him. Now the tiny
flame between the logs was burning brightly. Carefully she spread a handful of dried twigs over it.
A small spiral of smoke went straight up, for there
was no breeze. . . . Steve's voice was so gentle.
Why was she so sure that underneath his placid,
silent manner there was so much deep gentleness
and sympathy? The way he had stroked the head
of the wild duck that was trying to dig its bill into
his hand before he let it go. The way he had carried her so lightly, stepping carefully as he waded
out in the stream. His hands were not very big. His
neck was creased with a network of fine lines, and
the skin was almost copper-colored. . . . For the
first time the twigs in the fire began to crackle. A
flame shot up. Still on her knees she began to
scramble for larger bits of dried driftwood, then she
re-arranged the logs so the fire would get more draft.
She looked down in the fire and wondered what
Steve had done when he was in the city. Somewhere
he had a boy. A woman living with him . . . might

in some ways be destroyed; her personality, her petty fancies would have to go; the only chance would be for a very quiet, steady, deeper acceptance and contentment.

"Look at the fire," she called out eagerly to Hubert. "How do you like that for a fire, and I did it all with my little hatchet." Still on her hands and knees, she smiled, looking over at him. Her face was black from smoke and her eyes were smarting.

"It's a swell fire. Steve himself couldn't do any better. Of course, you had to work your way up to it," he said, still puffing at his pipe and laughing at her.

Hesitating a moment she said, "What do you make of Steve?"

"He's so inscrutable, it's hard to make anything of him."

"In some ways he reminds me of you. Do you know that?"

"Good. How?"

"You're both quite different persons, but in some ways you might both have had a drink out of the same fountain."

"The old, far-away fountain," he said, laughing. "But any kind of a drink would do now. I wonder if Bousneau has anything."

"Let's ask him." They got up and walked up toward the house. It was getting dark. "It must have been funny for Steve's wife if she ever lived up here with him," Marion said. "I'd like to have heard him talking to her for an evening. Of course he oughtn't to have got married. You can see that, looking at him. If the woman loved him, she ought to have loved him and let him go."

"I've thought about that, too," Hubert said quietly. "You almost put your finger on it. A woman really wouldn't be having an affair with Steve at all. She would be having an affair with this country, see?" he swept his arm toward the river.

Bousneau and the electrician were in Peter's room and they had talked till they were all sleepy. The electrician, who was glad to be back in the country, and who kept on repeating that any one who tasted the waters of Lake Superior was a prisoner forever, had a sleeping bag, and he was going to spend the night on the sandy bank of the river.

They had company next day, too. One of the contractors from the Falls, a big, deep-chested, generous fellow, and an engineer from Chicago, a kind-hearted British gentleman with a huge, red, British face, an immaculate gray business suit, a pearl-gray fedora, shiny tan shoes and, of course, a camera and a pair of field glasses, came down to the Mission to see the people from the city: they were both deeply disappointed that they couldn't be helpful. While the contractor talked sociably and good-naturedly to Peter, the British gentleman asked to be allowed to go rowing with Marion on the river. First he removed his coat, but he did not roll up his starched cuffs. On the river they went round and round in a circle because he wouldn't admit he was much stronger on his right oar than his left. When he was tired he rowed to the bank and took a picture of Marion with an immense rock as a background. Then they went back to the boarding house and up to see Peter, and the amiable Englishman told three jokes from *Punch,* the London paper, as he laughed heartily.

After they had gone Peter said vigorously, as though he had found a new interest in living, "Imagine a guy like that up here in these wild Algoma Hills telling jokes from *Punch* and wondering why we can't see the point. But it makes the point clear. Those jokes from *Punch* make it clear how far away Europe is, eh?"

And the very next day the blue-blazered Englishman came down on a truck from the Falls and was almost breathless in his delight at the conversation he had about High Church matters; he said gravely that English writers like Chesterton and Sheila Kaye Smith, who had turned Catholic without first securing an honorable peace between the Roman and Anglican communities, had committed intellectual suicide.

"Why bother me about such writers? They don't interest me," Peter said rudely, and the smooth-cheeked young man was offended and worried. He wanted to get talking to Marion whom he thought more devout than the others. "You know," he said to her, "you might make a convert out of me," and as she smiled, looking at him, she thought it almost her duty to do so, he would be so much happier.

So they had company, a kind of comic opera company, Marion insisted, and much conversation.

One day just before sundown, Marion, alone, went trolling with Steve. Hubert remained with Peter. Slowly he rowed her down to the mouth of the river and turned west where the sun was hanging over the far blue hills. When they were past the black rocks at the point, she let out Bousneau's line and watched the tiny piece of red rag and the white feathers spinning far behind till it was out of sight in the deep water. They were going past the dock. No one was at the warehouse. It was calm, smooth and peaceful on the water, and she smiled at Steve, who smiled and kept on rowing. Just before sunset, when the hills were so very blue, with bright patches that looked like cultivated meadowland with the sun shining on them but were really only places where the timber had been burnt clear of the rock, she looked at Steve and thought it was almost a quiet, holy time, a time for a close communion with some one. She looked at his brown hands on the oars and marveled at his solitary peacefulness. She liked his brown neck and the way he smiled at her so quietly. Bareheaded, she sat in the boat, her fingers holding the line, trailing in the water. Once she looked away shyly when he saw her moistening her red lower lip as she regarded him. Her heart began to beat so loudly she was afraid he might hear it, and she wondered why she should still be afraid of herself. Then the line was tugged off her fore-finger, tug, tug, tug, tug. "I've got it, I've got it, it must be a whopper"; then there was no resistance at all on the line; the fish was swimming with the line as she pulled it in. Eagerly they both waited. The excitement was so strong in her, her arms were trembling. Pulling in steadily, she saw through the clear water the sudden gleam of a silver white body, and just when she was ready to give the last jerk to the line it began to fight, tugging till the line cut her finger and she looked around wildly. She wanted to give the last jerk but the heavy line was so tight she could only hold on. Then the salmon trout leaped clean out of the water, the sun shining bril-liantly on its dripping scales, and it fell in the bottom of the boat, flopping, swinging its strong tail, flopping under the seat and back again. She tried to hold it with her hands and fell to her knees, then leaned back with her legs stretched out stiffly to feel it under the seat, its twelve-pound salmon tail slapping the bottom boards. Steve got hold of it, and she held on to it, too, and he grabbed his heavy knife and thrust the blade deep in the head between the eyes. It lay still. One of the big hooks was caught through its mouth and eye. Marion was so weak with excitement she could hardly breathe. Her face was white. "It's better sport without using the net," he said, smiling and beginning to row again.

They went far past the harbor and in closer by the high, overhanging, rocky shore to pass a small island, bare black rock swelling up out of the water. Three white gulls were on the little island.

"I like you, Steve," she said, smiling nervously.

He seemed to be startled. Finally he said, trying to find the right words to conceal any thoughts he might have, "Thank you, Miss Gibbons."

And she was silent till they were far out on the water again and could see beyond the low hills on the shore. She wanted very much to be like him; nothing she had ever thought seemed so important as her wish to be like him. The golden stripes in his sweater were very bright in the sunlight. "He's watching me. Oh, why does he seem so melancholy, yet so content?" Lazily she looked away, but deep within her was an uneasiness that seemed to hurt her.

"I've got a kind of pain in my side," she said suddenly.

"Did you hurt yourself?" he said anxiously, looking at her with his wide-open, soft brown eyes. He seemed to have so much sympathy and warm tenderness.

"No. It'll go away. It just got me when I breathed deeply."

Idly she looked over beyond the rocky shore to the highest hill. There was one great mountain with slopes so immense, the timber seemed like scrub on it. The upper slopes had been burned by forest fires, burned to the rock, and the timber, yellowish white, bare, stuck out stiffly from the rock like a jumble of match sticks, and beneath this burned timber was always the rock, slabs of quartz, basalt and granite, and the peak looked so white in the sunlight; it looked like an immense, crude, rugged cathedral of rock with deep, dark crevices for a decorative pattern. The peak gleamed so whitely. . . . As she dragged her hand in the water she imagined herself trying to ascend that vast sweeping slope, and it seemed that within her there had always been a mountain, and she had always wanted to feel herself on the white peak looking down the vast slope. For the first time now, looking toward the shore, she saw how far up and unattainable was the peak. And so it amused her to think of her mother and the young officer who had been killed in the war, and of Peter, always resisting and dreaming of his new world, and of herself, all starting to ascend the vast slope. The only one she ever knew who had gone on steadily was Hubert, but she was sure if he could see the mountain from the water as she was seeing it, with the peak so far away in the sunlight, he would go no farther. She glanced at Steve, who was looking out over the water. "Why does he make it all seem unimportant?" she thought, for his utter tranquillity disturbed her. She wanted it and wanted him.

"It will soon be dark, Steve."

"I'll turn back now."

They were a hundred yards from the point at the

river when she felt the tug at the line again, only
this time the fish did not swim with the boat; there
was a steady, fierce insistent tugging, almost jerking the thick line out of her hand. "Try and land it
over the back of the boat," he said, with as much
excitement as though it were the first fish he had
ever caught. So excited was she that in pulling in
the line she dropped it over the side into the water
instead of into the bottom of the boat. She waited
to see the gleam of the dark-bellied, silver-backed
salmon, but she saw a darker fish, and as she jerked
up, it hit the side of the boat and flopped back to
the water. "It's probably a pickerel," he said. "Let
me get the line," and he dragged in steadily to try
and land it over the boat side. He made a sudden
grab for it as he hoisted it out of the water, but it
swung clear over to the other side of the boat.
"We'll not land it like this without a net," he said.
"I'll pull it in from the shore."

Between the dock and the side of the point
farthest from the river mouth was an inlet with a
small sandy beach. Marion kept the line tight while
Steve rowed to this beach. The pickerel, pulling
strongly against the boat at first, suddenly began
to swim with it. A few yards out from the beach,
Steve jumped into the water, and Marion, standing
up, handed him the line and waited; he was going
to pull the fish out of the water right up on the
shore. Staring at the water, he pulled faster, as it
came closer. Inert and yielding, the fish swam in to

the shore, into just a foot of water, its body dark against the light sand. But when its mouth was almost lifted out of the water, it swung its tail against the sand, jerking its mouth from the hook. It swerved out to the deep water. "Damn it all," she said. They seemed to have been deceived by a carefully premeditated plan. "I knew if it got its tail against anything, it would get away," he said.

"Let's sit here on the beach awhile before we go up the river," she said.

After beaching the boat, they sat down in the sand. "We'll sit here just five minutes," she said, feeling afraid of the silence and the twilight. She was afraid, yet looked at him boldly, her lips parted. But now she was afraid from not knowing what might happen to her. As he took off his hat, his black hair fell loosely on the lobes of his ears. Helpless, he looked at her, not knowing what she expected him to say, and when she saw that he wanted her, she closed her eyes, trying to hold herself together.

"Kiss me, Steve," she said, leaning to him.

Timid, he kissed her and looked at her shyly. The smell of the water and the woods was on him. His breath smelt of pipe tobacco. "Oh, kiss me again," she said. "Kiss me hard." And so he kissed her as if he had become sure of himself.

She wanted to get up but her legs were trembling and she could hardly move. When she got up so quickly he was puzzled. Frowning, he said, "Won't we stay here?"

"No. I said I'd be back before it was really dark."

"I thought we'd stay here," he said, smiling patiently and looking so glad. "What are you afraid of?"

"I'm not afraid, I tell you. I love the fellow who was hurt. You know that, don't you?"

"I guess you do," he said, without looking at her.

"I'm just waiting for him to get better, that's all," she said rather childishly, as if talking to herself.

"He'll be better soon, won't he?"

"Yes, I'm just waiting because I love him so much. Well, that's all," she said uncertainly as she walked toward the boat. "I don't know why I've got that pain in my side." And she said to herself, "I guess I just feel nervous."

On the way up the river they were silent as though nothing had disturbed them. It was just dark. They could see the lights in the row of houses. Instead of asking when she would go trolling again, Steve merely smiled at her peacefully and had his own thoughts.

The brothers seemed to resent her staying out so late. As they both looked at her with a kind of mild wonder she put her hand to her cheek and it felt hot. She was angry with herself for feeling uneasy. Smiling, she kissed Peter lightly and said, "I must go and get washed for dinner."

It was almost dark in the room. "Your hands feel so warm," Peter said.

"Your head is just wonderfully cool," she said, hurrying from the room.

Peter said to Hubert, "I think we're losing our girl."

"What's that?"

"I think we're losing our girl," he said with a strange sincerity.

"Not Marion," Hubert said angrily. He added, "I don't like hearing you say that." He didn't like his brother, who was helpless for the time, talking so lifelessly.

19

THE following day the steamer from the Soo docked in the harbor. Indians from the reserve came over in old canoes, to sit all together on a log, watch everybody, and grin contemptuously. One long canoe carried six young children and a middle-aged squaw with a wide, ridiculous, Victorian, velvet hat, who paddled lazily. Trucks came down from the Falls to be loaded with supplies. Bousneau returned to the boarding house with a letter for Marion: Mrs. Bousneau, handing it to her, would have liked to talk about Peter, the very jolly young man who made fun of her every time she went into his room. The letter was from Mrs. Gibbons, who wanted to make an explanation. In the simple, straightforward, sincere letter, Mrs. Gibbons said she had decided to go away to France within a week, and remain there, if possible, the rest of her life, or as long as she had money. It was a crazy notion, she admitted, to want to spend the rest of her life near the place where her young officer had been killed and buried, but it would express the only notion of loyalty that was left to her. She was fond of Marion, she said, but felt that even she would find it easier if her mother went away.

Marion tried to tell the two brothers about the night her mother and the young officer had walked into the orchard, and they had both felt so close together without even speaking or moving. "That was the last time she ever saw him," Marion said. Her mother bewildered her: she went to her own room to think of her, but the more she thought, the more her feeling of bewilderment became a feeling of wonder. She remembered clearly that last glimpse of her mother when she had seemed to be suffering, broken and close to despair. What had so suddenly strengthened her? What was she holding on to all the time that now gave her fresh animation, Marion kept asking herself.

And Peter was saying to his brother, "What a young woman Mrs. Gibbons must have been. She still has so much passion and so much courage. I can't help liking her, and I can't help thinking about her, though I don't like talking about her with Marion. Is that the noise of loading down at the dock? Will the boat go soon?"

"I heard they expected to leave about five o'clock."

"I'd rather not hear that boat going. I heard it coming in. I heard the whistle and I started to wish it would stay at the dock for a long time, or till we all went back on it. I wanted to go back on that boat. It's hard to fight what you can't see. Lying here day after day I've been feeling terribly passive and unresisting and it's not my nature to be that way, I tell you. If I were around outside I'd soon change everything. I like to fight and be decisive. Here I just talk and talk and talk. I've been here trying to resist with my whole being something that's outside the window, in the noise of the river running and the lake and in the very silent nights . . . something I can't touch and can only feel. It's something I know I longed for. It still seems wonderful, and I feel almost mean and blasphemous to be resisting it now. I'll resist, though." His face got red. He started to lift himself up on his elbows. "I could get up, you know," he said. But he let his weight sink back slowly and screwing up his eyes, said quietly, "It's different with you, Hubert. You're so pleased with the world and you have such a happy acceptance of it. The world's your oyster and you seem downright surprised to discover anything can go wrong. Why can't you do something?" he asked irritably.

"I can do this. I can tell Marion you were wanting to go back on that boat."

"Please don't. Promise me you won't. I wanted her to suggest it. All day, before the boat came, I was waiting for her to suggest we go back, and I'll wait till she does. Anyway, I've sense enough to know it's futile trying to change things by running away. I don't really want that. I would rather have come up here than anything else in the world, so until she's ready, I prefer to stay. I think I hear her coming. Remember, keep quiet."

In the evening after dinner Hubert asked Marion if she would like to walk down to the dock with him and talk to the warehouseman. They took a lantern

and he held her hand as they walked down the
rutted dirt road through the woods. She watched
her words as she talked with him and looked mostly
at the circle of light the lantern threw across the
road. And even he wasn't talkative; he just held her
hand tightly. The light shone on leaves curled up
with dew. They heard the waterfall up the Magpie
River. When the road turned out of the bush to the
beach and the warehouse, they stood still and looking up agreed they had never seen so many stars or
such a night. The sky powdered with stars seemed
so high yet so dreadfully close; the stars swarmed
in an arch across the great water. They were walking ankle deep in the sand to the warehouse, where
there was a light.

"Such nights. Such nights, they destroy us," she
said.

"Oh, no. They exhilarate me. They make me feel
that we're really all magnificent and that there's no
struggle against life."

"They fill me with wonder, then they make me
feel afraid, because they destroy us," she said.
"They crush our resistance and destroy us."

In the warehouse a lean old man, in a dark blue
shirt with light suspenders, was sitting by the
lantern on a desk. He was glad to see them because
they would make a conversation. His face was
small, cheek sunken and leathery, but his blue eyes
were brilliant. He asked if they had any store
cigarettes and the three of them sat by the lantern

and smoked. For many years, ever since they had traded in this country, his family had been here, he said, and he had prospected and lived in the woods. He owned thousands of acres of land along the beach, with the best gravel in the whole wide world, and he was merely waiting for the day when some city contractor would discover the quality of his gravel. Or he would even be satisfied if some one would discover how to remove the sulphur from the iron ore, so it would be commercially profitable, for the whole country was one great piece of iron-bearing mineral, he said.

While he was telling them that he had spent years on a lighthouse they might see by looking far down the shore on such a night, they heard wild laughter and shouting along the beach.

"There they go," he said. "Every time that old boat comes up here somebody brings liquor and they get girls from the Mission and go crazy along the beach."

"Let's go out and listen," Marion said.

With Hubert she went down to the beach and along toward the point where the laughter got much louder and they could hear voices. Some one, a woman, went running along the sand in the moonlight, and a heavier figure, lumbering after her, caught her and hauled her down. She shrieked wildly, then laughed and was still. All the dark figures on the beach seemed to shriek together, then laugh hysterically. They would keep it up all night.

"Let's go down and crash the party and get a drink," Marion said.

"Don't be crazy, Marion, you don't know what might happen to you."

"Oh, come on. You're with me. We might have some fun."

"No. Go if you want to, but I won't take you." As he glanced at her he saw her shrug her shoulders and twist the corners of her lips scornfully at him. All the earnest faith and confidence he had always had in her seemed to be leaving him. She was looking at him, thinking him a prig, and sneering as they began to walk along the beach. But she said quite mildly and gently, "I saw a red-winged blackbird to-day. It swooped low over Bousneau's shed and the sun glinted on its wings."

"They're fine, bold-looking birds, aren't they?" he said eagerly. "To-morrow I'll show you a tree where I've three times seen a beautiful orange-feathered oriole. It's often hard to see them as plainly as I've seen this one."

She was walking with her head tilted up a little, taking firm strides in the sand as though her nearness to the swarming stars almost stunned her, and she said breathlessly, "Here on the beach at night it's so beautiful, the water is so vast, the beauty is so vast, and when I think of the low swoop of that red-winged bird, we seem so puny and inconsequential."

"It all belongs. Remember you're a piece of it, too."

Laughing she said, "Part of the godhead, eh, you sweet metaphysician."

"You don't need to be a metaphysician to see that your loveliness is a part of a greater loveliness," he said very earnestly.

"You lovable kid. Are you making love to me?"

"No. I'm reassuring you."

"Thanks. Then you believe in God, eh? And have faith?"

"No, for me it's a simple matter. Surely you have faith in something, Marion?"

"Yes, you've got to admire loyalty, and believe that it's in people, or nobility, or courage, even when you wonder whether such virtues touch your own life at all. My mother's religious faith has made it possible for her to live because she can go on hoping. That's the one thing she's got that I haven't got. Otherwise I suppose we're a pair. What makes it so easy for you?"

As they turned up from the beach he began to say with some embarrassment that one Sunday morning he went into a church because he had been walking and was tired. He sat in the pew, listening half-heartedly to the minister, feeling the soles of his feet cooling. The minister was an extraordinarily fluent man, though very unctuous, one of the most prominent divines in the city, a great educationalist. His voice was so nicely modulated. So he sat there listening to the minister and feeling all the time like giving him a big horse laugh. Suddenly, the minister said, "Can you feel God?" The words may not have had any relation to his sermon, just a professional phrase. "I was alert suddenly," Hubert said, "and couldn't sit there any longer. My thoughts were all mixed up and when I was outside I was repeating the words. The words just seemed to offer an intimation that bewildered me. It was very hot outside, yet I began to stride along the street without having any idea where I was going, as if I had a knot in my head and if I kept on moving it would slowly untangle itself. I must have got on a street car. Anyway, I was soon at the north end of the city, past the car line, and still walking along. I turned down a cinder track that led to a river flowing by an old paper mill. I remember clearly standing on the bridge opposite the tall chimney on the paper mill, and then looking down suddenly at the shallow river bed. The water was muddy but I could see the stones at the bottom in some places. And while I was looking down at the water this thing like a knot in my head was suddenly unravelled. I had a really swell feeling of elation and extraordinary clarity. There was clarity and unity and I was a part of the unity. The water, the banks, the old paper mill all seemed so perfectly co-ordinated by the feeling of spontaneous elation. I clutched the bridge railing tightly and was very happy. Maybe it was something like the feeling people used to be able to get by praying in very old churches in Europe. It was such a grand feeling. . . ."

"A regular Pentecostal feast," she said.

"I don't quite know what you mean, Marion."

"Sure you do. Didn't the Holy Ghost descend in tongues of fire?" she said a bit jeeringly, hurting him almost deliberately. Then when he was silent she said, "We ought to have gone down and joined the party on the beach."

His notions of what were best and good seemed to be slipping away from him. The basis of his life was being destroyed because he couldn't go on feeling sure of people. When he saw her shrug her shoulders, he opened his mouth awkwardly, then said savagely, "Listen here, Marion. Don't get things twisted up. You're probably fed up and tired and you've looked forward to everything eagerly and now you've been disappointed, but you've got to hold on to yourself. You might as well get this straight too; this isn't one of those affairs where the guy you're crazy about is permanently crippled, or frozen from the waist down so that it's necessary for you to starve yourself forever. It's just a little while in this case. You've got to wait such a little while, that's all."

"For heaven's sake, keep quiet. Don't lecture me like that."

"I'm not lecturing you. I was just saying it was a little while. I've wanted to say that and many other things to you."

"Such a little while. Isn't all of life just a little while?" she said, for the moment trying to spite him.

Then, feeling ashamed of herself, she took hold

of his arm tightly and they began to walk back, and she did her best to tease him, for she knew she had upset his faith in every one. Before they left the beach they saw old Jacob, an Indian from the reserve, sleeping under his canoe. A small fire was still smouldering. The old fellow didn't even look at them. First he had built a fire and let it warm the ground, then he had moved the fire so he could lie down on the warm ground by the new fire.

20

MANY times in the evenings she went trolling with
Steve. She got the notion into her head that the
brothers were standing aside, watching, and their
attitude irritated her. At twilight one evening
Marion came into Peter's room to sit down a moment. She was wearing a blouse open at the throat
with a little black tie. The brothers looked up as
if they had been talking about her and at once she
felt irritated. Usually Hubert irritated her because
he was so unconcerned about matters that seemed
to her to be important, but now at least he was worried. Looking at her shyly, he seemed to have lost
all confidence in himself and was waiting for her to
hurt him. Peter had his head turned to the white-
washed wall.

"What a sad-looking pair you are," she said in
her deep, husky voice, turning down one corner of
her mouth as she smiled.

"Hello, Marion," Hubert said.

"Hello, hello, Peter."

"Hello."

Laughing easily, she seemed to feel contemptuous
of both of them. The two of them were trying to
find strength, were trying to hold on to something
they shared between them in that little white-
washed room. She laughed deeply, thinking with

real amusement that all they had to do was go outside and they would soon lose it. They had both become a bit ridiculous. Though Hubert was sitting
some distance away from the window, she felt that
they were both really huddled close together. Yet
she went over to the bed and kissed Peter and ran
her slender hand gently through his hair. "Let your
hand rest on my forehead," he said. "Why?" she
asked so swiftly. "It's cool," he said and his lips were
twisted as he tried to express indifference and a
complete independence. "You must get better soon,"
she said with a light graciousness, though her
thoughts were not of the room at all.

"Where are you going, Marion?" Peter said.

"Just out. I asked Steve if he would go trolling
for an hour or so."

"He will, of course."

"Oh, yes."

"The fishing wasn't very good last night, was it?"

"No, so Steve rowed me up the river for a while."

"We're keeping you," he said. "Go on."

"Would you rather I stayed here with you?"

"No, please go on, Marion," he said. "There's no
purpose in your sticking here. I'd be very unhappy
if I didn't think you were having some fun."

"Good-by, you dear pair," she said, laughing
easily from the door.

When she was gone Peter said, "I thought she
might possibly ask you to go with her."

"Oh, no, she thinks it's better for me to keep you

company," Hubert said, trying to convey in a few words that at least that was the way she had felt about it in the first place.

"Can you see her going down the path from the window, Hubert?"

"Yes."

"Where is she going?"

"She's going down to the little landing by the water. She's walking slowly. She tossed a couple of stones she had in her hand at the water."

"Is Steve there waiting for her?"

"Not exactly. He was cruising around in a circle. It's him all right. I can see his sweater. He waved his hand at her and is coming in to the shore. I guess they're not going to use the rowboat to-night." Hubert came away from the window.

Finally Peter said to his brother, "What kind of a guy is this Steve? I haven't had a chance to talk to him."

"A very solitary fellow, seems a bit melancholy, but sure of himself. But Marion's wrong about him," Hubert said eagerly. "She thinks he feels alone. He doesn't feel that way at all, I'm sure. He's just become perfectly a part of this country. If you don't like the quality of the country, you don't like him."

"Does she ever talk about him? She talks about the quality of the country."

"Hardly at all, and the country seems to puzzle her."

"Well," Peter said, "it may be all right, but I hate to have to lie here and watch it going on. I just have to listen and think, and watch her, and not move at all."

"I think I'd better light that light," Hubert said, and he got up and went over to the oil lamp. The Mission was in the deep river valley where it got dark so quickly. Outside the sinking sun was shooting streaks of light across the mouth of the river, but it was dark in the room. "Don't light the light," Peter said.

"Why?"

"It's better in the dark. I can hear more sounds. I'm not so much just in the one room when it gets dark."

They were silent. Peter was thinking of the way she had looked on their second afternoon at the Mission when she had come into the room in her riding breeks, with her blue beret and yellow sweater, a woman so utterly apart and beyond the country; he had held his breath when he had seen her, and hoped she would always be that way, utterly apart and beyond the country because of the strength of her own independence. And then he wouldn't let himself stop thinking of this picture; every time it faded, when he heard the faint lapping of the water, or heard Bousneau talking quietly to the electrician downstairs, he concentrated and regained the picture; he knew that as

soon as he lay back and relaxed he would stop thinking of her and would feel the sinking, depressing
heaviness inside him till it would seem unimportant whether he ever got up from the bed. Finally,
when he couldn't go on thinking of her, he tried to
see the face of Hubert who was sitting in the corner
away from the window. His face was shadowed.
Shadows were dark in all the room corners. Soon it
would be the full dark. Hubert was sitting like a
man who had selected a foundation for a tall struc-
ture and having built, he sees he has selected the
wrong material. Hubert seemed to realize that his
own judgment had been faulty, and so he felt helpless, without any confidence in himself. Without
that cocky confidence, he thought he couldn't live
at all. "I guess there's no objection to talking, is
there?" he said.

"Why should there be?"

"None at all. I'm going to light the light. I won't
seem to be dissolving so completely if I see the walls
of the room at least," he said. He lit the light and
pulled down the blind and looked quickly at his
brother. They smiled very peacefully at each other.

"With the two of us here in the room, I don't feel
so bad," Hubert said.

"Why should you feel bad, Hubert? Of course,
that's probably the trouble with us. When the two
of us are together in a small white room we don't
feel so bad."

"No. I just wish you'd get well again."

"I'm getting better. I'll get up soon. I know I won't be able to walk right. I know it."

"If only you were well again."

"But I've had to lie here and watch her going away, watch myself losing her. It's very funny. You lie here and after a while you don't resist, you almost feel steadier, or even stronger. But you don't resist because there's something so inexorable about the place. It's not so much the big, quiet river, or the lake, it's the primordial hills and the stillness. I believe it's a kind of grandeur, not the grandeur they talk about finding in Shakespeare's plays; that's something like some of the sunsets you've been telling me about. It's something more quiet and more steady, and more inexorable. It's odd. Well, you said a moment ago something about dissolving. It's funny to feel and hear and see a person's identity dissolving, going to pieces, and you can't do anything about it."

"Maybe."

"No. I didn't want to say quite that. In your own head, or inside you, there's a picture, or notion, or ideal, of some one and then you lie on your back and watch it destroyed. It's the destruction of the character."

"I wish you'd lie still, Peter."

"Oh, I will. But here's a joke for you—I've always been so eager to get right down close to the root of America, eh?" he said, smiling. "You can't beat this country for that, can you?"

He lay absolutely still, with his eyes closed, and he did not open his eyes for a long time nor make any move of his head. A few feet away from him in the old rocking-chair, Hubert, with his long legs stretched out, looked steadily at the clean, whitewashed walls, and sometimes at the uneven flame in the lamp. Once he even began to rock in the chair, but he seemed to become remarkably interested in the worn, colorless piece of carpet covering the wide boards on the floor, and he stopped rocking to stare down intently; then, as if he had tried very hard but had seen nothing, he looked up, glanced at his brother, whose eyes were still closed, and he began to look patiently at the walls again. Every springtime Bousneau did the walls freshly, but from the heat in the chimney in the winter and fall, the thick whitewash flaked easily and fell. Just below the window there were voices, a low, old woman's voice and a man's voice, people going down the path to St. Leo's store, and there was a great rustling on the water and in the trees as if the wind were coming up. If a wind came up the waves would pound steadily on the black-rock shore. From far out on the lake came the cry of a loon, a long, quailing cry. Downstairs Bousneau, playing cards with the electrician from the mines, began to laugh heartily, a loud, rollicking, helpless laugh, as if he could only shake his head and go on laughing. But back of the house, at the shed, a mongrel began yapping and Bousneau thumped heavily across to the back door and yelled angrily at the dog. The two voices that had passed by underneath the window on the way to St. Leo's store returned, passing slowly, like old people, and only one voice was raised now.

The lake water, despite the low rustle of the wind in the trees, was absolutely still, and the river water made no sound. The two brothers remained alone in the room, with the oil lamp burning, without talking at all.

21

WHEN the motor boat curved around the point, heading out to the lake, Marion noticed, smiling faintly, that Steve was sitting well back huddled over the engine, in much the same position he had been in the first time she had seen him, only now he was smiling and not shy at all. As if it were very important, she carefully let out her line, then looked at him intently. The great lake was glassy on the surface that had the color of the dark rocks and the western sky. Way over along the shore past the Dorree River the land jutted out into the lake and the sun was dipping behind those hills, hanging first like an enormously swollen orange, then sinking across the greenish, misty, opalescent sky, down behind the purple hills. It was dark soon on the water. The engine fluttered rather futilely. Behind that far outthrust arm of land and its high hills were many brilliant-colored sashes on the sky, as if just over those hills at this time there were a more grandly operatic world. She thought vaguely of the two brothers back in the small room in the boarding house on the river.

"Steve," she said suddenly.

"Yes," he said gently.

"Will you ever go back to the city?"

"Not likely," he said, smiling slowly. "I may go down to the Soo once a year or so, but the city is too monotonous."

"Will you ever get married?"

"Who will I ever marry up here?" he laughed out loud.

"You'd better not get married."

"Why?"

"I don't like to think of you being married."

As she was talking she was feeling weak and dazed. She had completely softened inside. She put her hand on the edge of the boat, wishing he would touch it with his hand. Not knowing how much he wanted her, she was afraid that if something didn't happen she would start trembling and he would notice her. "I've got to, I've got to," she said to herself. He was curving the boat in a wide arc and looking out over the water. To have something to do she began to pull in her line. Her lips were parted, she was feeling almost numb, and when he wouldn't look at her she felt glad, for she knew the feeling that was inside her was inside him too.

Finally he said, pointing across the water at the small island of solid rock, a hump on the water with a bit of scrub on it, "Can you see those three loons over there, just off this end."

"No, I can't, Steve."

"Keep on looking. There, you can hear them now."

One laughed long and ridiculously, but it seemed to startle Marion, the lake was so quiet.

"I certainly heard that," she said.

"They nest over there," he said. "They are big strong birds."

They would become silent easily, so he began at once to talk about the loon's nest, his voice soft, pleasant and polite. "They have very strong, powerful bills," he said. "They could thrust a hole through the bottom of this boat. Other birds leave them entirely alone. Last summer an Indian boy from the reserve along the lake thought he would swim out from the shore to the little island and take the loon's eggs from the nest. He was a strong young boy about fifteen years old and very gay. He swam through the water quickly and the loon noticed him coming toward the little island and her nest. The loon flew overhead till the boy got close to the island, then it darted down under the water, stabbing with its bill. The boy was a strong swimmer but he screamed and was helpless as the loon stabbed him in the body; they are used to doing that; they fish that way. The boy was stabbed and killed. He was drowned. They never got his body."

"I don't like that story. The boy was too helpless," she said.

"He was."

"It's terrible to be helpless and not able to resist. Then you get so that you don't want to resist."

"What will we do now?" he said. "It's getting dark. There aren't any fish to-day."

"I don't know. What'll we do, Steve?"

"Will we go over there to the shore on the little beach by the point. We'll sit there together on the beach. I'd like to do that. Will you, Marion?"

"All right, Steve."

He kept on looking at her so steadily and gently and was so sure of himself. Her thoughts were all mixed and she knew only that she was glad. They didn't speak while the boat was headed toward the tiny harbor. It was getting dark quickly. Eagerly she looked at his brown face, his hands and his neck. She was not afraid of him, and not afraid of herself.

On the beach, washed up logs were floating in the water. Carefully the boat went through these logs, the nose of the boat just pushing them aside. Steve jumped out, balanced himself on the logs, and tied the rope around the tree so he could pull the boat farther into the shore. He helped her out and they went walking along the beach, their shoes sinking in the sand, their bodies leaning forward.

"We'll sit down here," he said.

"All right, Steve."

"Do you like it here?"

"Yes."

She seemed to want to do just what he told her. He put his arm on her shoulder. He kissed her clumsily and hastily, and she was bewildered be-

cause he didn't go on kissing her. She closed her
eyes. Then she said desperately, "Oh, Steve, let me
go."

"No," he said.

"Please, Steve," she said, without moving at all.

"Oh, no," he said.

"Oh, Steve, please, Steve, Steve."

Then all the feeling went out of her and she felt
only disappointed. Out on the lake it was quiet with
the moon shining palely. Logs on the water kept
bumping lightly against the side of the boat. The
logs kept on bumping, that was the only noise. He
was beside her, crouched on the sand, feeling awkward and uneasy.

"We'd better go," she said, brushing the sand
from her blouse.

"All right, Marion," he said, speaking so softly
and caressingly she could hardly hear him.

With a sudden tenderness she said, "Kiss me just
once, Steve." And she kissed him lightly and got
up and walked down to the edge of the water. He
held two logs together with his foot so she could
get into the boat without wetting her feet. Balanc-
ing himself on the logs, he pushed the boat out,
stepped in, and huddled down over the engine, alone
now, and apart from her and yet content. She felt a
strange impersonal tenderness for him. As soon as
the boat got off shore she felt cold and began to
shiver, then she began to cry quietly. He knew she

was crying but didn't try to disturb her by talking
to her. His head in the moonlight looked more
melancholy, more solitary.

"Don't mind me crying, Steve," she said. "It's all
right."

"I don't mind," he said simply.

When they turned the point to go up to the Mission on the river she was facing the wide, dark lake.
Now the disappointment was so heavy within her
she was afraid to speak to Steve. She didn't want
him to notice her disappointment. Once she turned
her head and looked up the river at the boarding
house at the light in Peter's room. The lights in
Bousneau's boarding house were much brighter than
the candle light in some of the smaller houses. On
the flat stretch of land at the top of the embankment was this one short row of lights and around it
was the blackness of the wooded hills. The put-pit-
put of the engine sounded loud in the river valley.
Slowly the boat curved through the thick weeds on
the surface to the frail old rotting landing, and Steve
held on to a post while Marion got out. He looked
up at her. From the bank she looked down at him
and smiled shyly. His face was full of longing for
her, as if he could not believe he would ever see her
again.

"Good-night, Steve," she said faintly, wiping her
eyes with a handkerchief. She wanted him to see
that she liked him and didn't blame him for anything that had happened.

"Good-night, Marion."

"Good-night."

He remained in the boat, watching her go up the embankment. Once she stumbled in the soft earth, her body falling forward, supported by her hands on the slope. She kept on going up, her shoes sliding, till she was at the top. Without looking back, she walked independently to the boarding house. It was not hard to follow her in the moonlight, but when she was in the shadows by the house, Steve couldn't see her at all.

22

MARION went into the house and spoke to Mr. and Mrs. Bousneau. "Good-night, Mrs. Bousneau."

"Good-night, Miss Gibbons."

"Good-evening, Mr. Bousneau."

"Good-evening. It's a grand evening."

"It's been a splendid evening," she said.

In the hall upstairs she saw the light in the brothers' room, but she went into her own room and sat down on the bed. She had thought of lying down on the bed and closing her eyes, but she sat there, still and erect, and in a quick moment it seemed that during all her life, rushing eagerly into a convent, and out again, always holding herself aloof from her mother's life, she had longed for purity, and now it was all sullied.

She muttered, "I'm no good, I'm no good, I'm no good. I'm no good. I'm no good," and bending down, holding her wrists between her knees, she said, "I knew all along I wasn't any good. All along, I knew in the city. I didn't know it so much up here for a time." Then she sat up stiffly with her head erect in the moonlight. "You knew all along, too, God. I wanted to come up here. Why did I ever come up here? I wanted so much to come up here. But I knew, God, as well as You did, so you're not fooling me."

As she listened, she began to think of the rotting wharf and the thick weeds. On the river in the evenings she had always been afraid of those thick heavy weeds on the surface. The first time she had seen them she had been afraid because the water was so dark underneath, dark and deep because you couldn't see it. Suddenly she got up and went over to the window and looked down the embankment at the river and the moonlight was on the yellowish weeds. Far down the dark water looked so smooth but there was the light on the yellowish weeds. . . . "I'm not afraid to do it. I'm not afraid," she kept saying. "It's what I ought to do. It's what I'm ready to do. Oh, why don't I do it?" Then she muttered passionately, "I won't. It will be better to know what I'm losing. I'll know, too, what I'm worth." And trembling she went back and sat down again waiting for the picture of the wharf and the weedy water to go out of her head; the picture seemed so much a part of her, so deep within her now, she could hardly put it away from her, and her head began to sweat. And she didn't know she was all right again till her body felt chilled, then she sighed, and was glad to feel herself crying a little.

Then she walked to the door and called softly, "Hubert, Hubert, come downstairs to the porch for a while. It's so wonderful out I don't like to go in yet."

"All right," he said, and she heard him getting up. He must have been sitting beside his brother.

When she was on the stairs, Mrs. Bousneau said to her, "Hello, there. I thought you had gone to bed."

"I wasn't sleepy," she said, "so I thought I'd get some more of the fine evening."

Outside, she stood on the porch waiting for Hubert and when he opened the door, the frame of his body looked so big and square against the light. He was smiling and seemed awfully glad she had called him. He was delighted.

"Do you want to sit on the porch, Marion?" he said.

"No. Walk with me a little bit, not down by the water, up toward the path and the bridge."

"Sure, that would be a grand walk."

When they started along the path, she said, "I didn't want the people in the house to see us, or hear us."

"Fine. Go ahead. I hope you've got lots to say to me. It's so long since we had a good talk, isn't it?"

Just as they were going up the little slope to the road, she said, "I was out with Steve to-night, you know."

"I know."

"Well, it's over. I let him make love to me. No. I wanted him to make love to me and he did. I've been wanting him to for some time. And he did."

Though her heart was pumping steadily and she could heardly breathe, she tried to smile and said, "So I'm no longer being saved up for the worms."

He stood still on the dirt road, kicking his foot at the wall of the deep wagon track, kicking, digging, and trying to find something to say that would make them both feel better. Suddenly he said eagerly, "Maybe it's better that's over. Maybe it's better that's all over. That never was so important. So don't feel bad about it," and he put his big arm around her and they began to walk up the road to the bridge.

"It's not that so much," she said. "But to be thinking a lot about integrity, and then discover that you haven't got it. . . . I wasn't thinking about anything else."

"Oh, you're right," he said eagerly. "You're a splendid woman. That's the way to look at it."

Just when they were opposite the waterfall on the Magpie River with the spray in an opalescent mist at the foot of the falls, she would go no farther. She put her two hands up to her face and was glad when he held on to her arm. "It's my lack of faith that's important," she said faintly. "I see it. My lack of fidelity, my lack of honor, and I haven't got those qualities."

"Don't talk like that, Marion. You're a fine girl."

"I don't seem to have had any faith in anything."

"Please, Marion."

"My mother is all right because she has faith, so

she had consolation. Everything can be forgiven for her, and she can be really sorry. And she isn't without honor, either. That's fine of her, going off to France like that. I'd like to go with her."

"If you'd let me talk to you for a while. I think you've always been a fine girl. I want to say——"

"But of course there's a nasty streak in mother and there's a rotten streak in me. I've always known how much alike we were. Years ago I felt it and tried to get away from it. I've always been trying things so hard. I wanted so much to come up here."

He didn't try to talk to her because he knew she had destroyed all his old notions of her, and destroyed all the things he thought important, and yet he simply knew he couldn't bear to lose her.

"Well," she said, more casually, and more brusquely, "you're a great boy, Hubert. I wish I could be like you, but I came out here just now to tell you this. There's a steamer comes in here to-morrow at about noon, you know. I'm going back on it."

"Oh, please, please, Marion."

"Yes. Peter won't be surprised. And it's better. It's better to leave the both of you for good. Think of what I'd do to Peter in the long run, going on without respect for myself. Oh, it's always been so uncertain, such an uncertain passion, like the big lake out there. You don't know what it will be like one hour after another. Why I'd probably be making love to all the men at the Falls. I'm going to-morrow."

Stooping down, he picked up a stone and threw it up toward the white falling water. "All right," he said.

"Don't be such a baby, Hubert."

"I'm not. Not at all. I just don't like to see you go."

"You two haven't got enough money. I'm going to pay Bousneau. Then I'm going to send money up here for the doctor. After all, it's been my trip."

"All right," he said simply.

Almost timid, as if it were none of her business, she said, "Is he any better, do you think?"

"He's some better. He thinks he'll get up soon, but he'll never walk right, he thinks."

"I mustn't talk about it. I mustn't or I'll go crazy. You tell him I'm going, will you?"

"No, you. You ought to."

"Yes, I ought to. I will."

They walked slowly in the dark down the path past the newly painted church and St. Leo's general store to the boarding house. At the porch Hubert said he would remain there while Marion went up and spoke to Peter; he looked at her like a big, bewildered boy who was trying hard to feel confident.

Upstairs she rapped on Peter's door and said, "May I come in?"

"Come in, come in, Marion."

She stood at the door looking across at the bed. "I'm sorry there's no light here," he said. "We were sitting here without a light. We got tired of looking at each other and Hubert blew it out. I'd like to see you. Why don't you step over there to the shaft of moonlight on the floor?"

"I'll stay here," she said.

"All right."

"Peter, I'm going back on the steamer to-morrow."

"Please don't, Marion."

"Yes, I must. I must leave you alone. I really must. It's over. I was rotten to bring you up here, but I looked forward so eagerly to coming. I still think we were right to come. Well, I'll go, and this beautiful country, this place where we wanted to be, will still be outside of us. It's still there, and so terribly real, but just outside of us. We wanted the right things, Peter, but I touched them and spoiled them. I hate to say good-by to the river and the lake and the hills. It's a grand night out, Peter. I mean it's like saying good-by to the very necessary things."

"I'm glad we came up here together," he said.

"Peter, listen to me. Steve has been making love to me. I've got to get out."

"I know. Or I mean I thought so."

"I'm going at noon time to-morrow. Isn't it extraordinarily light here? Did you ever see such nights?"

"I've been able to feel them here."

"That's right. You can feel them every bit as well as you can see them."

"There's been hardly any wind on the lake for days," he said.

"Oh, please, Peter, try and get better."

"I'll try," he said.

Before he could really see her, she moved close to him, kissed him, and moved back to the door. "Good-night," she said.

"Please don't leave me, please don't leave me, Marion," he said, sitting up in the bed. "Oh, please don't go away."

"Peter, Peter, good-night," she said.

She went back to her own room and began very methodically to take off her sandals. She put her sandals close together just under the bed and began to pull off her heavy stockings. Two burs were stuck in the wool and she pulled at them very earnestly. She heard Hubert coming up with heavy steps to his brother's room, and then, when she listened she heard their voices murmuring. In the next room they were talking steadily, but she couldn't hear anything they said. Then she decided not to undress at all and she rolled back on the bed and closed her eyes, thinking, "It didn't just happen to-night. It's been going on slowly, and I've been knowing it." The notion of going away, which from the first had been consoling, now began to excite and strengthen her. She felt eager to go, eager to scourge herself by leaving so much behind. "I'll leave Peter, dear Peter. I'll leave this strange country. I'll hope to gain something." But her whole body felt lifeless and cold as she thought, "If only we had had one night together. Just one night together."

The night was chilly. The nights remained clear and brilliant but they got chilly, and she was pulling the bedclothes over her body.

23

IN the morning Marion got up late, long after Hubert and Peter had had their breakfast. They heard her hurrying downstairs and talking to the Bousneaus, who were disturbed because she was leaving so abruptly. They heard Mrs. Bousneau rattling a frying pan in her determination to give her a splendid meal, and Charlie Bousneau was shouting that he himself would row her over to the dock. The Bousneaus were taking it for granted that she had to get back to the city and were promising to give the young men splendid attention, so they would want to come back next year.

From the window, looking down the river, Hubert had seen out over the lake the smoke trailing on the sky, and later on he had seen the steamer pass the river mouth. Much later he was still sitting by the window, when they heard Marion hurrying upstairs, Bousneau following, to get her bags.

In a rush she opened their door and thrust her head into the room. Her fair hair was brushed back behind her ears and her blue beret was on one side of her head. Her face was powdered carefully, and her lips were red and well marked. In her arm she was carrying the light coat, and she was wearing the little blouse with the black tie. The brothers looked at her, solemn and wide-eyed, and Hubert got up awkwardly. "I'll go down with you," he said.

"No, Charlie Bousneau is going with me. You stay here with Peter. Good-by," she said.

"Good-by," they both said together.

"So long," she said, waving her hand at them and smiling gayly. There wasn't much to say, because Bousneau was standing behind her in the hall. They heard her go out and then they heard Bousneau talking under the window as they went down the embankment to the wharf. Three short blasts of the whistle came from the steamer over at the dock. "He wants to hurry," Peter said, "or he'll miss that boat."

Hubert watched Bousneau rowing her down the river. He stayed at the window and watched them turn round the point, then he went over and sat beside Peter. "I think I was trying to tell you what Mexico would be like," he said, and then his voice trailed away and he was silent. They felt very close together, very necessary to each other in the small, white room.